I0725655

Victimless Crime

Jeanette Powers

No Dying Allowed:

I'm sleeping on the couch and I'm biting my nails. The thing about my nails is that I don't bite them like everyone else. People bite the tips at the white part and then just kinda keep going at them down to the quick. Then their nail-tips are like tiny islands with rat-tooth shorelines and it's not attractive. Not attractive at all and when your fingernails look like that, everyone knows you are totally a real nervous Nelly. You are certain to have "too much baggage" or "be a nervous wreck" you are certain to be "extra." Course I'm not really sleeping, I'm lying here in the dead silence and picking.

But anyway, I don't bite my nails like that. My nails grow long and seem to naturally have a French manicure. The color of them changes so dramatically as soon as they aren't connected directly to a blood supply. You never saw a thing change so quick. Soon as they're dead cells, they've got nothing to them but white decay. Funny how people see the dead souls hanging from your fingertips as something to be coveted, as some sign of "I'm better than you" or "I've got my shit together." When I bite my nails, it's along the edges, not the tips; I chew down deep into the root cuticles. I know once I get an angle on something to tear, I won't stop until I can rip it the fuck out.

Then it's a problem solved. I'm all craters and ridges.

When I bite my nails, everything gets more streamlined and I carry clippers because if left to my own devices, I won't stop until I tear that hangnail all the way out. And by out I mean down. From fingertip to rounded cuticle edge to first knuckle and sometimes it just bleeds embarrassingly and I have to suck my fingers and knuckles into not bleeding out anymore.

Did you kiss it better?

It's all about applying pressure. Until you push hard enough against the red river inside, it's a flood plain. Flood pain. Then I'm jealous of the shoreline nail biters; I'm a tide of blood.

It's dark outside and there's a light winter rain, it's fucking cold this year, the whole GD river is an ice skating rink. No ones knows what to do about the world. The penguins have to learn to live without igloos. Van Gogh died penniless and unknown. The center cannot hold and things fall apart and all that and I can't sleep and it's a long night gonna fall. I know I should relax. I don't fucking relax ever. I can't find a good way to lie on the couch. The pillow has changed. It isn't the same pillow it was before, but simultaneously I've lived with this pillow for two years, and nothing has interfered with it. No aliens. No washing incidents. No Chad fucking Smith asking for open mouth kisses and then insisting. Nevertheless, the pillow changed one day. Without permission and now it's shitty and I'm salty about it.

I move the pillows around every day. This is a persistence of my daily routine. Which pillow is the one that doesn't make my neck hurt? Well, it doesn't help that they are changing every day. How can a scientist observe a system when that system has no internal order? Really no self-respect at all! One day soft as goose feathers. Goose down feathers, the good shit. Next day it's like burnt marshmallows, and that's where I'm supposed to rest my head.

Well, it's a shit show.

The point is not the pillow. The point is not my chewed nails or the tiny cuts all over my body from the busted safety glass. The point is that I'm laying on a goose feather bed of nails and I'm twenty feet away from someone who may or may not be dying and by dying, I mean killing themselves. Could be alcohol poisoning, could be the just-one-last-time shot and nod away, could be he hung himself again. Could be something brand new he's thought up, he's a mad genius when it comes to self-destruction. He is in there right now. Behind a single door whose lock I definitely know how to break.

It's up to me whether or not I break through their door and check his pulse and save his life like a super-zeitgeist like Seabeck did last time and then we'll all stop tearing into ourselves, or not.

✶✶✶✶✶✶✶✶✶✶

Once, I was in a new town and now that town is old to me and everyone else. I was happy because no one would know me and I was incognito. Everybody would be looking for somebody and I would be nobody, no strings, no history, no seven-degrees-of-sexual-intercourse. Of course I went to a used bookstore slash bar, I can be in love with an infinity of books because they are full of everyone's imagination and I love that. But there's this poetry reading going on, Blue Mondays, and even though they're all like victim-porn or healing shit, I stay. This old lady is hosting, she isn't wearing a bra her hair hangs like swamp moss, she looks mean even with the gold toothy grin. Her name is Sharon and I tell her I don't want to read when she passes me the list. I always remember how at the end of the night she looked me in the eyes and held me by the shoulder. She said it was a pleasure to meet me.

I don't know why I got cheeky. I say *oh yeah?* and she just smiles and says

"Everything changed. I like it."

"To new beginnings" and we raised our glasses to each other, thunked a corner of the thick glass on the bar top and drank. I always remember that, some people you can just remember the exact moment you ever met them. You don't know it then, but you just never forget.

Anyways, it's easy to meet people at Blue Mondays because the thing about poetry readings is that everybody comes alone because no one has friends who love poetry because it's like totally circle jerk on parade, totally extra. And the infernal snapping and honestly I don't actually understand a word they're saying and it's no surprise none of them have friends who will come. Why do I keep going fuck if I know.

That's where I first saw John. God he was actually ugly, and definitely full of shit. He's floppin around talking about being molested by his 7th grade boy scout gym class priest or whoever and how that's why he shoots up heroin with the French Bitch and not one person buys this show. This is why he aint on Broadway. He's a fucking shitshow. And he's got the most beautiful strange cheekbones. It's like they gave up and just fell down, like they trace gravity to the center of the earth, he's a real flatface. Blonde. Blue eyes like sewer water reflecting the sky. Big teeth, very white a sign of being rich. Later, we would postulate that he actually had undiagnosed fetal alcohol syndrome. He tells everyone who can hear that he's from *New York Fucking City* and goes intermittently in and out of an east coast accent. He's basically the illegitimate love child of Andrew Dice Clay and some druggie beat poet everyone claims to have read but actually haven't. Later I would learn this character is Jim Carroll.

Heyheybae? Tell me again about the private jet that flew you and your family into KC and delivered you and the household goods to Merriam County where the well-to-do know how to do well and do. Tell me again about how you are from Port Washington Long Island which is to NYC what a 2008 Dodge Grand Caravan is to a '18 Fiat 124 Spider. He's a fucking suburbanite, born and bred, just really a rich kid silver spoon jackass slumming it to piss off his parents. Course, I didn't know all that then. I just saw a beautiful abomination wailing about a trumped-up assault because he was trying to fit it with all the lesbians.

The first time we played video games together was the first time he got pissed at me. Rage. Course there had been plenty of rage before, but like the kind I thought of as healthy, like a nice anarchist vibe of destroying plastic planters with the chain and padlock he kept hanging from the shoulder strap on his leather jacket. He'd show off to everyone how he could unsnap quick at the right side and swift would the heavy chain drop into his hand and his grin would shake with his head bobbing up and down with the camaraderie of violence. We'd be real psycho shitstorms together and go in for some low-grade property destruction of corporate offices or terrorize Scientologists by putting "No Aliens" stickers on their van or yell *fuck Palestine* at black Jews on street corners with battery-powered loudspeakers who believe Beyonce is the devil. We'd paint ourselves up like circus clowns every night and just go antagonize the city.

We hated the world and I thought that was because of the world's injustice. It was that for me, but for him it was just the hate of love. Whatever wants to be liked, he hates, whatever needs to be hated, he hates. His love is reserved only for the mild disinterest of the psychopath. His idol is Roger Stone, his favorite movie is American Psycho, his dream job is used car salesman, his favorite novel is some Spanish magical realism where the violent protagonist romanticizes that the best way to kill himself is to kill everyone who'd ever loved him, that way his memory would be eradicated, too. I guess the book must be a sequence of watching the light in the eyes die of everyone who ever made the mistake of loving him. This makes sense for John, he thinks this is the highest art, he calls it what the author called it: *the duende*.

John never really came up with anything on his own. He does not create, he only destroys. And his destruction is so hungry. He is starving to death.

But so the first time we're playing video games, it's Wii Bowling. We swing the white, wireless dildo-jobbies and made the ball bowl and it was my game system so I was winning. He missed the split and the game made the *wah-wah* sound that screamed to John, *LOSER!!!* and he just fast-balled the remote against the wall and after that we didn't play video games anymore. Instead, we smoked in the mudroom and I asked him if he was seriously so angry about losing a video game. He said *no*, and that was the first of many lies. Apparently, it was high art for him to lie, too. But never really about what he did, always always about who he is.

I'm struck awake by a loud man's voice I don't recognize. It's still dark. My face is pressed into the bad pillow and in John's room he is using his new blue-tooth speaker to blare a youtube video on cannibalism. He's alive. It's not like telling the Donner Party story or a movie starring British people. It's a man and the poor audio of a cell phone camera extolling how to cut up women into the choicest bites. It's serving suggestions and recommendations on what to freeze and what to eat right away. I hear the man talking about how old-fashioned it is to consider eating beautiful women to be cannibalism, that that word doesn't apply to what delicacies he creates. I can easily hear the man from every room in the house and I can't help myself for listening.

I want to yell at John and ask him to turn this shit the fuck off. I also don't want to make a sound. I also don't want to draw any attention to myself because this is a new development. I mean he stopped eating food really a couple months ago. He's a GD skeleton. How hungry is he in there? What's he drinking? What's he holding?

These are more questions I don't want the answers to. This list of these questions grows. Who's he talking to?

I turn on the Mountain Goats and the song sings "I hope I lie and tell everyone you were a good wife. And I hope you die. I hope we both die." It's on my daily playlist and I know it's one of John's songs he loves to sing when he's sitting in his car and chain-smoking with a handle of McCormick's vodka. I save it to my private playlist so I won't forget what he means. I think there might be some exit, he says there's no exit. He says there's this one spot on the bridge.

One day we were panther cuddling on the smoking patio at Buzzard and hollering at each other in a way we considered the good side of abandonment: having abandon. He spilled the last beer and I kicked the can into a curving waterfall on the floor. "You are fucking worthless" I tease. We'd insult each other with vast pleasure usually, but something was different that day, with what I'd said. He turned storm dark, vortex dark, black hole dark and his chin met his chest and he glared at me from under his brows. He said, "don't fucking ever say that again. That's what my father says to me." He leaped across the bar stool, picked me up and threw me to the floor. We loved it.

Then he started choking me with the scarf I was wearing. My eyes bulging at his green docs, my face planted in the ashes and butts because everyone just flicks and stubs at the floor. The old slated laminate wood grooved into my cheeks and his knee was in my back.

Not being able to breathe is not as scary as I thought it would be. It's not as bad as this interminable indecision about whether or not to try and talk to him, to see if things can be saved or are going to be burned to the ground. Right now at least I know he's not dead the cannibal is talking about stuffed green olives right now. Frannie thinks it's strange I can tell my stories without weeping. Bukowski would not have found that strange, not him, not his blue bird, they don't weep, do you?

I pounded my fist on the ashy bar floor calling *uncle*, I always want to live. There's only three rules between me and John. The first rule is *No dying allowed.* I wish the floor had been a mirror so I could see his expression. Was his face indifferent? Flushed? Was he experiencing joy? Terror?

He always told me after that it was nothing but a game. But I knew how he felt about losing.

Rule number two is *No dating.*

Rule number three is *No duking in the bed.*

It's a fucking metaphor, and that's why they call it *eating shit.*

Here I am dreaming of myself. I'm in Vegas, it's the desert and there is only one high rise and that's where everyone does everything. I walk out the front doors, the greeters don't know how to say good-bye and I walk into the burning sand. At my left is a full moon and at my right is a setting sun and in my forward vision is a world-ending asteroid and it's coming straight for me. The burning comet hits the atmosphere and sharply angles its trajectory. This is a trick of the air. It burns a pillar down to the ground where I stand. I'm somehow myself and also simultaneously able to see the curvature of the earth running away from me. All of the dry sands are set on fire and the world turns to transparent glass and the high rise building falls and everyone is screaming dead because they thought they were safe inside, but actually I was the only one who lived because I ran into a burning bush.

I'm not dreaming, I'm awake. I'm awake and shake the pillow I know that is true because nothing is burning to the ground and the world hasn't ended and Vegas doesn't have one high-rise, it has a shithole of high-rises and I put the music on loudly because I'm not sure but I think John's masturbating in the bedroom because I heard him mumbling and moaning when I went to piss. His light was on and the youtube videos are still playing and this time it's some southern dude talking about the top five most fuel-efficient cars.

Now I know he's not dead. I'm sure he heard me piss and flush and there's no avoiding the creaking of the hardwood floors. He'll surely come out sometime because he's not a piece of shit, he's just a *trashperson* and there's a difference.

He's probably texting with the Des Moines girlfriend. I wonder if he's telling her that he has to cum quiet because his wife is home or if he lies or if he says nothing and I know all of this is a fucking waste of time because he's into wet holes and broom-closets and I'm into not vomiting or masturbating in the bathroom after fucking and I don't know how to tell anyone the truth about that.

Fuck the pain away. I wish.

Whatever, he's alive.

He could just walk right out.

Yesterday afternoon he told me he's afraid to actually meet her, because he's not really into any of the things they talk about during their phone sex. I don't want to hear about any of this shit because he's been checked out for 6 months, but I only became aware of this in the last week and we broke up less than twenty-four hours ago. It's a fresh fucking wound to me and I'm all broken wide open still but he insists "I just want to be honest with you about everything" and so he goes on about his and Des Moines bitch's fantasies.

"She wants to fuck me in that motel on the Iowa/Missouri border where I almost got a DUI." This is the motel where our relationship nearly ended and probably should have. I was in Vegas and he was on a three-state bender, to see some other random woman. "She thinks it's funny to fuck there because you were so upset about me getting almost arrested." Why is he even telling this new Tinder match about that fight? What a freak.

I could go in there and fuck him now. Instead I stare at the cracks in the walls of the old house. I'm not a state and a half away, I'm lying on the couch in the front room and creepy listening for whether or not he's alive or dead. I could burst in and throw the phone out of his hand and put my ass in the air and he'd forget all about whichever her he's doing phone sex with and he'd put it in me and she'd be listening on the line still and he'd scream out about how he loves my pussy and how I'm the only one he wants to cum in but what he means is what old biker bitch Sharon always says: "I love you when you are with me."

I'm sure they're both drunk as fuck because it's after midnight and I just don't have the energy to fake another orgasm so he'll think he's special so he'll think he should keep loving me so he'll know I'm sexually available because that's the deal if you want to be in his life.

He's alive and the worst thing about that is that it makes me free. I don't have to keep sitting shiva with Schrodinger's Dummy in the bed we used to share. He's alive and nothing is burning down.

There is only myself to reckon with. I chew on the edge of my right hand thumbnail and stare at the places where the wall spackle looks like a laughing toothless woman made of salt.

✶✶✶✶✶✶✶✶✶✶

I'm on the couch and I'm trying to masturbate without porn so that I can fall asleep. I'm not really sure why I took all the porn apps off my phone except that when it was there I didn't look at anything else. Stoplights, intermissions, bathroom breaks, just desperate women with desperate trans-femmes of all ages baring their pimpled asses or stretch-marked bellies and dinner plate nipples or tiny caged lady-penises in attempts to get sexual attention, to feel adored, subjugated, or be forced, feel his surrender and then be on top, to make someone cum so you can be on top of the food chain for the minute they are completely consumed with shattering orgasm.

So I'm trying to masturbate and all I can remember is a photo of this youngish woman from clavicle to mid-hip and she's in front of a window. Actually, I don't know their pronouns, but it's definitely tits and a slit. The sunlight is highlighting the inner edges of their thighs. The pubic hair is full and a tiny happy trail exclamations to the sternum. One hand is holding up a white t-shirt. This is innocence, and I imagine them sitting on my lap. I imagine asking permission for them to lift their shirt, for me to caress their small breast.

So I'm trying to masturbate and they're on my lap but all I can think about is my first boyfriend's dick in my mouth and how badly I was sucking it. I mean, I was like 15, what did I know about sucking dick? But I was sure I was bad at it because that was before I watched porn and I had no fucking idea what I was doing. But he definitely wasn't SKEET SKEET SKEETing in my mouth and so I was failing. I didn't know then to tease and lightly teeth with a corkscrewing head and busy tongue. I didn't know then to give myself a concussion by looking up into his eyes and moaning while I pretended to gag on his HUGE HUGE HUGE cock.

I'm just a kid and this fucking 45-year-old mummy-dude has got me by the short and curlies because I've got like daddy issues. You know? He's way too fucking old for me but that's what you get for meeting shitbags on Craigslist. Also, maybe motherfuckers got

Daughter Issues. Like old dudes gotta bang young chicks because they can't just be a good person for their kids, so they convince themselves to go out and take care of some neglected teenager with tiny tits and a shaved head. I didn't have but one stick and poke then, but I was covered in scars from where I'd take child-safety scissors and tear apart my inner bicep, soft white thigh, ankle bone. Because you can't tell me something is safe without me proving you wrong.

But also, you can't tell me something is dangerous without me trying to show how I can best it.

Now it's after one am and the youtubing is replaced with the sound of texting. *Bloop bloop blip blip* announces another new text every couple seconds. It blasts through the blue tooth speaker obnoxiously. Probably he's trading nudes with some woman who lives in Baton Rouge, or the little whore in Des Moines. They'll have raw-dog sex in a car parts store parking lot and he's proud about how all his texts and selfies have got him moving up what he calls "her penis ladder." This is fucking sickening to me, and I called him a *fucking-worthless-trashperson* when he told me. But she's there in some other town and he's here with me and not with me and it doesn't really matter, and I let him do it all to me because it doesn't fucking matter. GD Queen taught us that, Freddie Mercury singing "nothing really matters" to a bunch of starving Ethiopians. Typical.

Well now we are both masturbating without porn, 'cept he's got a live catfish and I'm working with some sorry dead worms between my legs. We've fucked enough for me to know I can't get off sucking his dick unless he's 69ing me, too. I have to be like completely distracted. I try thinking about sucking him off. Fuck, I don't want to jerk off thinking about him, I think of a gang bang from congressmen instead. I get shoved full in every hole and crevasse because my whole body is one diamond core drill. *Vroom Vroom.* Cuts the uncuttable!

Wish my grass was EMO so it would cut itself.

I'd probably come so much harder if I plugged my fingers into my ears while his dick was pounding my gag reflex and his right hand was bludgeoning my pussy and his left hand was flirting with my asshole and even harder if you came along and pinched my nose together and suffocated me to fucking death. If I could get every hole filled at once then surely this GD brain of mine would finally shut shut shut the fuck up.

I pull my fingers out of my slit and sigh. My long middle finger nail is cutting my hood. Sex is violence. I remember the first time a man touched my asshole. It was my step-father, his name was Gary. He snuck into my room late at night and laid next to me. I woke up, but it was weird. I didn't know to be scared yet. Since I didn't know why it was happening, I kept pretending to sleep. He moved his hand along my waist. I was afraid even to flinch. Then he moved his hand up to my bitty 12-year-old tit.

That's when my degree in acting was granted. I rolled over to press my baby breasts against the dollar store sheets and took a different kind of sigh, very convinced that this would convince him I was asleep. Who would fondle kiddie tits while the girl was sleeping? If he realizes I'm asleep, he'll obviously stop.

Who would fondle a sleeping baby girl?

This is a typical 12-year-old thinking. I didn't know what consent meant then, but I knew what it felt like. So then I'm belly pressed into the cheap sheets and pretending to breathe normally while Gary is breathing heavily into the back of my neck.

That's when he went for my ass.

I'm not checking on him and I'm also not texting Frannie. This is my mantra for the early hours of the night. Frannie is always trying to save me, nevermind that her life is way more of a wreck than mine. Once she threw away all my clothes and bought me new ones. She told me "no more velour, ever!" And she was right, I looked and felt much better when I had her style.

The first time I saw Frannie she was 21 and walking into the Cajun restaurant where I worked. She was tall, thin, perfectly proportioned with dark hair cut into a bob and a distinct pep in her step. A real pep-stepper! There was a caged brilliance in her eyes. She saw the whole room at once, she did. And she took control of it while all the while looking like a punk rock bimbo Barbie doll with accidentally somehow brown hair. If you looked close, her eyes were flat brown and she wore an inch of foundation because her skin was so bad. She was a picker and the more you looked closer at her the more gross things you noticed which was prolly why none of her boyfriends lasted more than two weeks. Dang, though, she was pretty walking through the glass door of a un-ironic mid-western oyster bar. She's still the prettiest thing there and that's like two years ago. We've bartended two Mardi Gras together now, geezus that's an epic fucking party. Last year it ended with us getting matching inner lip tattoos. Time's gotta way with going light speed and also with keeping us landlocked.

So anyways Frannie walks through the greasy fingerprinted glass doors and step-peps behind the fat ass manager and looks around at her first day on the job. Every last damn diner sees her. The fish in the fish tank see her, Olaf and Carl see her from the server station. Jose and Tio see her from the kitchen, the GD hand drawn tacky jazz portraits stapled to the walls see her because she is the most unmistakable woman you've ever seen. 14-eyelet green Docs. Mustard yellow tights. Denim short shorts and an AC/DC cut up shirt with an upside down flaming cross.

I'm behind the bar at the *glergh-glerghing* frozen drink machine pouring just one more Bermuda Triangle alcoholic-kool-aide-horrorshow with three straws filled with liquor (silver rum, spiced rum and dark rum) to a Rex Simon, who I know has taken three Xanax before coming up to drink and Rex and I see her and I think, "damn, that girl is my new best friend."

And she was. She saved me a bunch of times from men, and that's why I can't text her now and couldn't call her about John Friday night, because she already gave me the ultimatum of the old *him or her*. John always said that best friends hate boyfriends, and he was right about that. But maybe it was just that best friends hate abusive fuck-wads. Basically I do just about anything for her in thanks for saving me so much, anything but actually leave John. I can see why that irritates her. There's only so much self-destruction a person can witness and keep watching, unless you're me I guess. I'm a bitter-ender.

Frannie has a mean streak, too, she aint perfect. She has a special way of humiliating me when we're out drinking together. If she hadn't drawn attention my ring, no one would have noticed my fat sausage fingers and then I wouldn't have had to tell the story of Vincent and his asshole jealous brother and all the rest. But when they noticed my worthless yellow-glass ring that meant they noticed my hand too. And beautiful Frannie couldn't help but turn her square jaw to me and mention about how she would never wear a ring on any finger because when she was in 3rd grade her teacher said "oh my what fat fucking fingers you have!" Or something like that and how now every day of every since and every sense beautiful Frannie has hidden her hands away like a good girl and made damn sure to stay thin so no teachers could ever call her fingers fat again.

Me, I was like, *fuck everyone*. I'm gonna wear this beautiful worthless glass ring. And when she saw my hands and then she told the story of her elementary teacher, I don't even think she knew why she was telling it, but I did. I had done something she would never do, allow my hands to be seen. And in a way, this gave me power. So I held up both hands and said, loudly, "Potato Eater hands, right?" And make everyone feel insecure for not getting the reference like I can never have skinny fingers. Tit for tat, yunno. She's prolly got GD shoreline fingernails too and I know her knees are covered in pocks from picking "ingrown hairs." I look to the Latinx woman, expecting solidarity. She's wide-eyed so I say, "Like Vincent van Gogh, the potato eaters in the painting got real fat hands like me because we're poor and we work. I'm a peasant."

The woman says, "Well, van Gogh lived off his brother" with this air of *he ain't shit.* But I know the story so much better and I've been dancing and feeling the top of everything as though my body is the melody and my hands are the high hat and my ass is the gut of the whoever wrote it and I was blind but now I can see and then the DJ played Weather Report deep tracks so I'm all flushed and grooved and yunno, just really can't be brought down by some beautiful girls because they're actually dull and my fat fingers can out drum roll them without even missing a beat of Stevie during *Superstition.*

So I say, "oh, you know the story? Vincent did live off his brother, Theo. And so you know Theo ran one of the premier impressionist galleries, breaking all sorts of now famous artists."

Frannie interrupts, "Break? what do you mean?" Beautiful though she was, thin Frannie was sharp as cutting board.

The Latinx woman says "you know, like a BIG BREAK, so you get famous."

I'm like "exactly. Theo made Degas, Manet, Monet all famous, but just hid away his own brother's paintings in the back office. No one ever even saw them! In fact, Vincent only sold one painting in his life, and that was to Edgar Degas. And Vincent died inside of shame, that he forever was an albatross on his brother's neck. And no one knows any of this shit except for that they lived really far apart and so had to write all these letters back and forth, and that's how we know what happened today.

"Also because this vicar wrote about Vincent. Because it was a small town, and the vicar loved Vincent and said about him 'you never saw Vincent with a whole crust of bread' because if he had anything he'd share it with a GD stray dog made of bones. But then he had to get shacked up with that horror fuck Gauguin who had a wife and like 10 kids but fucked them all off. Original absent father, and ran to France and then to Tahiti where he basically raped a bunch of native girls and we're still paying to see how he painted their naked, abused bodies and we're all like HOO FUCKING RAH, this shit is awesome.

"Fuck that dude. Anyway, Vinnie is living with Paul and Vinnie loves this whore. Because you know, a poor, fourth daughter of a serf family in 19th century France without being Frannie-beautiful aint gotta lotta options besides selling her slit. But Vinnie knows her true, like they look at the irises in spring and shit together. And Paul's like, 'that bitch don't love you, she'll fuck me for two coins.'

"And Vinnie says 'no way', and of course the whore fucks Paul for two coins and Gauguin comes around with a wet dick and fingers smelling of whore quim and Vincent says 'I won't hear that story.'

"And that's why Vincent cut off his ear and sent it to her in a cardboard package delivered by the post."

Now everyone's real distracted from my fat fingers. I'm good at that, because it's that or actually be like some fucking anorexic and I really like beans and eggs and cheese and eating and I don't even like men or sex that much so fuck the world. Everyone's kind of silent and I can tell I've talked too much again.

"Vincent couldn't afford turpentine or linseed oil, so he always wetted and cleaned his brush with his tongue and teeth, so he got lead poisoning. That's why he killed himself, I think."

Or maybe he killed himself because everyone was always betraying him? Bringing his brilliance down. Erasing his shine. That's not why John's trying to kill himself, he doesn't care about living off his parents fortunes and he doesn't care about the whores, he's trying to die because it'll piss off his mom, I think.

No one can save him.

✸✸✸✸✸✸✸✸✸✸

I wake up and my fat face is pressed to the pillow. Corduroy creases edge into my face and the house is silent now and that means he's dead in the next room. Like 55% dead. I mean likely dead at 55%. I don't want to go into his bedroom. But you know he's gonna kill himself any day and seriously though not on my watch, damn. I press my head harder into the pillow. It's not comfortable.

He's dead. I'm here. He's not dead. It's just like my fucking aunt, yunno. That's why she drove recklessly and recklessly is the nice way of saying *she drove herself on purpose off a cliff.* Everybody passes out with that much dilaudid. So she's dead, he's dead. He's definitely dead. He knows all the percentiles of how much when and

boom

done. He's prolly in there dead now. What if he went out while I was asleep, then I wouldn't know what he drank or scored. I'm not going in. I check the fridge, nothing moved. Trash either. All the same as last night, I think. I'm pretty sure. I'm not hired to check on him. This is not my job. I'm stamping my face into the pillow until my name is a vice grip because I'm powerless as he twists the bar of me tight. Until he strangles me with my own scarf. Which he can't do if he's dead in there and if he is then there's the whole explaining to his mom about how we didn't really get a divorce last year but got a kind of continuance and he's been lying to her about where he lived for the last year and it was with me and I'm calling her in 20 minutes because John is dead in the bedroom.

I'm sure of it because this is surely his fate, he's been telling me for so long about the ideations. The feeling worthless and hopeless, the last book of poetry, the spot on the bridge, the kiss off to his rich parents, the burning apartment, the duende.

His mother'll be proud of his corpse because he's the thinnest he's ever been. She'll be angry with him because there will no more weigh-ins when he's dead. My fingers are all scabbed over.

I take a piss and memorize the arrangement of hairs and wadded toilet paper and razor packaging in the bathroom trash can. He shaved his legs sometime yesterday. For Des Moines, no doubt. For sexy time.

It's nothing.

Nothing.

Just facts. He hasn't left the house, he's still here. I'm just going to drink a little more whiskey and then close my eyes for one minute.

✶✶✶✶✶✶✶✶✶✶

He will. He'll. Hell. Heel. This is John over and over. John has made a mission of finding hell. He'll surely will himself to Hell. His favorite pro-wrestler is Ric Flair, his favorite politician is Roger Stone. He loves it when Woody Allen fucks children. He coos with delight when Trump tweets. He secretly listens to Alex Jones at night and is developing a greater sense of hating women. These alt-right suck-holes are teaching him great and strong men who-really-know-how-to-do-what-to-do all agree that women would be able to make good decisions if they had a dick. Of course, they also don't let transgender women use the women's restroom because males wanna do nothing but rape rape rape. It all makes good sense when you're rich and white. And he's white and he's rich and he just wants his birthright, you get it.

He's started saying things like: *You know what the problem with black people is? They don't trust financial institutions, if they just got a bank account and didn't bounce their fucking checks they'd have good credit and get off welfare, and I'd rather be a misogynist than miserable, and it's one or the other with these fucking #metoo bitches and yeah I'm a proud ableist, you know why? I'm not a cripple.*

But then he also wants to die in a gutter. Sycophant. Hard to do with your world-class health insurance and endless source of funding called *daddy*. John blames the world for him not getting his big break and becoming a famous poet and his college rival, Ernie Fuckin Holmes, got the special class with Irving or whatever-white-dude professor they were all hard-on about. Now John won't write a thing. He just spends three hours a day parked in his running car in sub-zero temperatures. He chain smokes and only has 2 Four Locos and a pint of whiskey most days. I can see him through the window, lifting the drink, lifting the drink, lifting the drink. It's like super systematic, almost robotic. I imagine what he is actually doing is two-fold: if he keeps drinking, he'll stop remembering how hungry he is and he'll pass out which is the best way to not eat. Also, he doesn't have anything to do until Easter, and so he's just passing time the best way he knows how. With a phone in one hand, his dick in the other and enough booze to black out nearby.

He's trying to get empty.

Easter isn't that far off, the first Sunday following the first full moon following the vernal equinox. Then after Easter when he meets his mother for early homemade brunch and his father for dinner out then the next time he'll have to pony up and actually do something won't be till the 4th of July, then Thanksgiving, granted no one is getting married in Fresno this year, granted that Memaw doesn't die this year. Sometimes a look of fear crosses John's face when his mom or dad calls in a time frame that doesn't make immediate sense. His whole fuck-you attitude melts nearly imperceptibly and once when the call actually meant his grandfather had passed, he wrote the most beautiful letter to his grandmother I'd ever read. Like big picture, you get it, it might have actually made her want to live.

He can do that with his words. And he hates himself for it because to him "hope" is the greatest injustice and he can't stop believing that cuz it's the first thing he learned as a kid.

I told him I was unlovable. Of course he didn't believe me, you'd have to be some sick fuck or some psychopath to believe it when someone said that and then be like "marry me". But it's true. There's something inside of me and everyone could see it from the first bawling baby breath in the hospital. I move too fast and learn too fast and call people out on their shit too much. I remember when I decided I hated my mother, I was four. She was fighting with her second husband and I was watching from the dark of a hallway. I thought to myself, "whatever happens in this world, I'll never be like her." And that's also when I knew I couldn't count on anybody but me, and so that's when I got so tough. And that toughness makes people fucking crazy. John calls it the afterburners of a jet engine, Frankie calls it a runaway train, Mel calls it manic, Bill started a fb group called "how to survive disappointing" me, Michael calls it cold, Jeff calls it "Galadriel's Light", Mark calls it juju, I call it *the robot*.

The thing about it is that I love the robot, the robot is a problem solver. Robot is what got me through my childhood alive because sure weren't any adult fuckers lining up to guide me, teach me, nothin. The robot is like *hey super ju-jitsu radical revolution I don't get told no*, but like, in a consensual respectful way where we are respectful of each other's boundaries and don't project all over each other. Robot's the reason I'm not another cubicle cog but am instead like whatever I am. Robot's the reason I'm at like 80% sure of convincing a tech mogul to let me man his private space plane in the next five years.

I always wanted to be an astronaut. Outer space is the perfect place for unlovable alien fucks who just wanna rocket the fuck outta here.

✶✶✶✶✶✶✶✶✶✶

I'm awake again and my heart bursts with fear of what I missed while I dozed off, but his car's still here so he's most likely in the bedroom still. I heel-toe to the door and now I can hear the ambient noise of youtube and because it hasn't stopped I can't tell if he's dead or not. I've wrestled the covers flat and I can't decide if I'm cold or hot and the inside of my mouth hurts.

We blacked all the windows out when the cold hit because John works nights and the house is drafty so instead of the clear shit we got full black plastic insulation and duct taped it down over all the windows of the house so he could sleep better and so the gas bill is cheaper. It's always about what makes him comfortable because he's the one willing to spend money on anything. Everybody knows I won't even turn the heat on past the lowest setting and only then so the pipes don't freeze. I like surviving to be a challenge. But it's so fucking dark in the house and he still hasn't come out.

At least there's no evidence that he's come out. I mark the median of his desk, I know the place of his phone charger. I keep tally on the content of the trash cans, all three. In the kitchen it's obvious he hasn't eaten because the top of the big trash is still yesterday's junk mail. In the desk trash is still the last two liter from the "Spanish sangria" he is always making and drinking but I also know that particular jug is two days old and I know he hasn't come out because there are no donut hole wrappers or used q-tips which jitterbug atop the plastic. Last is the bathroom trash. There's more here to investigate than trash, but also there's no q-tips, no tooth-picks, no snot rags and most importantly there's no wet floor mat, no dusting of humidity evidencing a shower, no tiny shavings of five-o'clock shadows in the sink, no eyeliner left on the counter. No nose clippers hanging around obnoxiously.

He hasn't left the bedroom at all while I was sleeping, it seems. So I creep to the bedroom door. I want to touch the doorknob to see if it's locked, but I don't. I have to not care. I have to not care if he's dead or alive because he told me he hasn't loved me for a year and that he has a new girlfriend and it has to be her job to check on him even though she's in Des Moines and we're a door apart in Kansas City. Even though I'm listening with all my might to hear a snore or a moan behind the simple drone of the mindless videos going on and on about the basic benefits of having a Camry instead of an Oldsmobile, or whatever. I hold my breath at the door so if he's alive in there, he doesn't hear me creeping. I'll sit by the door only one more minute. Sometimes the minute takes an hour.

It might be forever that I can hear the shows on spool, it might be only a moment but it feels like more than I have to give.

It's cold and dark and that's what I think is the purpose of love. I tell Frannie all the time that love is pain. She thinks I'm fucking damaged. Nothin another shot won't solve.

Everything is so much more complicated and the fact is that everything could explode at any minute. Like the Tacoma Bridge collapse, youtube that shit. They built this heckin rad new bridge, and like week one, a gust of wind just right comes along and just busts it the fuck up. Like the way an opera singer can shatter a crystal wineglass. It's called *resonant frequency* and sometimes I feel like this waiting is doing the same thing to me. Any minute the build up is going to blow me apart. I know it will because Henri told me so. Henri Poincare discovered this and that makes him the greatest mathematician of all time. Sure, other folks did whatever rad ass shit. Newton and principia, Albert and relativity, Feynman and building the bomb, yeah that's all he did, ha! Unified fundamental forces. Descartes put everything on a grid and function. A language of the calculus. Fucking beautiful. Sagan and ET and DeGrasse and whatever he talks about to the kids these days, but Henri, he's the true great.

He did the kind of calculations which take a computer all of its focus, but he did them in pencil with like log tables and shit. Total psycho shitstorm maths. So he's looking at this three-body gravitational problem that arises when you take Newton's gravitational derivatives past two-point interactions. Easy. Sure.

No. Henri keeps getting these crazy world-ending results. Orbits shattering like wine glasses. Like, no matter what, everything is bound to go to hell in a handbasket no matter what we do or know. He mathematizes that inevitably and without warning the entire universe will unhinge in its orbits and spiral out into total destruction. Of course it will. Duh. Don't forget that even though we can't predict when it will be, it is guaranteed that it will happen.

Ha! LMAO! Told ya'll mofoes! Corrupt system. Implosion inevitable.

Luckily we aren't made of explosives.

We're made of energy, and energy cannot be created or destroyed.

✶✶✶✶✶✶✶✶✶

I'm exhausted, just facts. I need coffee, so I grind the beans for a really long time because it makes so much noise and maybe he wants some coffee, too. He bought me this coffeepot. John does nice things for me, actually. Also, whenever anyone says "actually" that's code for "there's more to the story." Learning to ask for the more story is an important advancement. Most of us aren't curious about the entire universe inside every other person that exists, most of us forget about universes that aren't our own. That's why so many old fucks won't admit they are racist, they can't even see themselves as anything but best intentions. Well, maybe your best intention is to keep racial purity, I don't know. I went to an Afro-Latinx show Saturday night. One poet spit about his tagging the world when he was a kid. He said "we reclaim the space that was taken from our ancestors. We paint souls where they build projects." I shuddered and shudder.

I don't have anything like their story, I don't fear for *abuelita*, for *hermano*, not like they do. I don't struggle like they do. What the fuck did I do for this break? Like everybody's just looking for their big break, and if anything I've fucked off the whole bit of privilege I was born to. The blood in my veins invented imperialism, colonialism, conquest. And I've been the sweet meat of their adventures. God white men they wanna jerk off on me so bad, I can't even imagine what it's like for an Ayala, a Garcia, or a Martinez. Whatever.

This is what dissociation is like. If I start thinking about everyone else, I disappear. I pour some of my desk whiskey in the cup too.

Last Monday, though, he did nice things for me. Took my car to get new tires and an alignment and we drove for like 10 GD hours to all the places, stopping in the cold and calling on the phone and harassing people and bartering for a better deal and *ohmyfuckinggod* in the end he decides that Walmart has the best deal with the best deal and are-you-fucking-shitting-me, of course they do. They are the Kings of the Undercut. This is exactly how mom and pop's get eviscerated. This is why capitalism sucks. OK so like Walmart is selling candy and Coke products at 20 cents more than everyone else, but everyone went to Wally World to get antifreeze or cat litter at the cheapest price around. But Wally World knows this is what you are doing, so all the splurge stuff is everywhere: corner displays, mid-aisle bins, the railroading egress to the pay station with the ultra-splurge aisle. It's seriously all like stuff you'd get out of a claw machine.

They are totally banking on your boredom. *Doctor Distraction, what is concentration?*

But if you are playing for the home team, the same thing is happening to me right now because I'll do anything to keep from thinking about how John sometimes does nice things for me. Because if I think of that, I might try to love him again and I am tired of plagiarist pillow streaks on my wet cheeks, and I'm tired of being afraid in my own home, and being told about how he's gonna kill himself every other day between eating binges (2 ravioli) and the inevitable hours of flexing gaunt muscles before the full length mirror and the inevitable sequence of youtube videos about the dark web and cannibalism, or whatever.

Still, this week he did a nice thing and I was exhausted. Later, after he'd drunk himself obliterated enough to black out he started wandering around the house and I spied. He just went to the pisser and bashed his head on the door when he tried to leave and he cursed a bit and he went back to the bed, slamming the door shut. At least he made it to the toilet this time.

I went to the bedroom door and listened as he went back to bed. Within ten seconds he's moaning orgasmically. Then instantly and fully he's coming really hard, like in less than 30 seconds. *Ohhhhhh, O O O Ohhh, gaaaahhhhhhhh,* some sort of *BRRRRR,* then full voiced: "Fuck those people in Detroit!"

He said that a few more times and the worst thing is I know he doesn't know what he's saying. So I can't help but wonder if he knows what he's saying when he says he'll help me. Or loves me.

But it's not like anyone else is offering.

Anyways, we never got the car new tires, Wally was out of my size. We just drove in a snowstorm for an hour and a half back home. The bitterness doesn't taste like coffee at all, it tastes like shame.

✶✶✶✶✶✶✶✶✶

I've been sitting outside his bedroom door so long now I feel like I should punch myself in the face. It's embarrassing, I am pathetic. The first time I punched a man in the face it was glorious. Me n Tera are standing on the deck under the outdoor heaters at Buzzard and this schmooze-fest fuckhead is towering over the pair of us and going on and on about how well he fits his knickers or some inane shit but he just keeps patting Tera's head, saying shit like *a good girl like you would do that, wouldn't you.* That's not meant as a question. And here's Tera all silenced and gulp full of vomit and fear and she's all wide-eyed and I imagine that's hot to him because he knows he's wearing her down. And really folks, is it a surprise that man is a predator? That predators are looking for prey?

What do you call a frat boy in a suit? *The defendent.*

And of course he guffaws some blow-hard woman-hating frat joke and *wakka wakka wakkas:*

"somebody should just punch me in the face!"

He's laughing like the big bad wolf in granny's bed. And if I'm being honest, I'd had just enough of all that. Of all the wide-eyed, closed-mouthed girls, of all the men towering over, of the nervous laughter over jokes about my tits and what I'm gonna put in my mouth if he buys me a drink, and what I owe him if he helps me with my computer, of the whole *can't you take a joke* routine and the moving my hand to his hard cock and the pressing the back of my head while I buck like a rodeo bull. Everybody likes to see that cowboy ride! Fuck everyone.

It was really so simple. He asked for it. So I reeled my right fist back swift as justice and KA-POW! That square jaw jerked back, his lips twisted and when he snapped back this look in his eyes! *Hee-Hawww!* O I can relive that moment forever. He was just so hurt, and I was ready for it. His little puppy eyes came round with a whimper of *whadidido?* and I just stood as tall as I am and said, "You should be more careful about who you tell to punch you in the face. Now go buy us drinks."

God did he hate and cower before me ever after that. I punched a bunch more dudes in the next few weeks, all for being frat boy fucks but in the end I just felt like I was getting high in the same way they did and if I hated them it was because I hated myself, and the same went for all the pseudo-victim women and that's when I decided once and for all that I was gonna go for a different kinda guy all together and that why I fell so hard for the junkie, for John.

The second time I saw him was at the intersection of Pennsylvania and Westport Road, where this street preacher was going on about abortion is murder and the junkie was in a pop punk pink polka dotted dress, a bleach blonde mohawk, black fishnets and eyeliner to match, smeared down his face and he was egging on this street preacher something fierce.

"Hey! and fuck the Muslims too! And the fucking democrats, Hillary for Prison!" and the street preacher is forced to agree with this abomination tranny throwback screaming at his feet. Legendary. The whole scene certainly doesn't impress any good Christians into finding their holy way in the drinking district on a Friday night. In fact, it just draws the police. Obv John can run faster than any of them due mostly to not having to cart along a portable amp and a mic but also because of all those soccer lessons from his days at private high school. So John is wailing and throwing himself on the ground and humping the street curb while he's screaming "save your skeet for Jesus!" And yunno I'm totally in love.

It's like everybody lost their guts along the way. Everybody lost the nerve to stand up for themselves, they forgot they don't always have to do what their told. And what a damn shame anyway because me n you know the best feeling in the world is reeling back and lashing out at the unjust, fucked up and also divinely gorgeous world which we are all missing out on because we're all afraid of the wrong things. Like you're over there scared of ever, like ever, seeing a snake and then you're over there maxing out credit cards and working a job you hate. Sucker. And then nobody wants to admit they're a sucker and it's really most everybody so then it's easy for the masses to just all band together and cry glory about malls and sky-malls and amazon fucking prime and each of them are shrines to Chevy over Volkswagon, are worshiping at the altar of which new bistro and vogue TV shows basically sucking the dicks of Coke and Windows, or whatever. Point is, now everybody's rally call is "Buy! Feed!" and what that translates into his "OBEY." And they do. And I have.

Of course I was raped. Everybody's been raped. Still a lot of everybody aren't admitting it yet, are calling it something else today and probably even figuring up that they think they like it rough and scary because otherwise it means that first time wasn't how it was supposed to be. Frannie says *we grew up indoctrinated by rape culture, of course it became our fantasies.* She's got a point. I was luckier than most, I just woke up and old boy was fucking me. It wasn't violent, per se. Yeah, I was a kid at that old flophouse and everybody knew me and I went to pass out in Chad's room and I thought that was OK. But I wake up and pump-pump-action-shot and yeah I lied there like a corpse. He left his own room after and we never spoke about it. Of course, I didn't give him much of a chance, I avoided him and anywhere he'd be after, like that was my job.

That's what all the girls did and still do, are you kidding me? It took me six years to tell anybody about what my step-father did and it wasn't half so bad. Except it was worse because it was in my bed, and I had to keep living with him, and he had control over my mom and told me what to do and then there was the whole worrying about whether or not he'd do it to my sister. And later, when social services made mom make him leave, there was the whole hearing about him marrying some other lady with a 12-year-old daughter. And I felt responsible, and then there was the whole being so fucking mad at my mom for not telling me that I could actually criminally prosecute him, and realizing she just let him go, all unaccountable but gonna ground me for smoking pot while she's drunk. Whatever.

I did what you do after Chad, he climbed off me and went somewhere else, I grabbed my shit, rinsed off in the bathroom sink with the hand cloth and drove my car home and snuck in the back door, like usual. I didn't know what *processing* meant then, but I did a hell of a lot of it the next day and here's what it boiled down to: FUCK EVERYONE TO FUCKING DEATH. Something made me feel less than, something made me feel I couldn't talk when those men were raping me and I didn't really fucking care what that was, I just wanted it to never happen again. And so I never learned shame, I learned rage instead. I decided to start screaming and punching men in the face.

And that's what I'm saying. Be disobedient. Get yours. Grow some guts. Don't take no shit from nobody, I ain't gonna get told no or told I have to no more. *You can't oppress me.* And I'll tell you what, having that in my heart has full-tilt made everybody afraid of me. Ain't nobody fucked with me really ever again, and I feel for those girls still getting fucked in the dark while they die inside, because I feel for me, too.

But, baby, we got a honey-pot full of dynamite but you gotta burn your hand on it and hold the pain to prove it's yours, and then nobody can take it.

So, okay, everybody is actually just about okay with living halfway. For instance, my college geometry teacher was absolutely not okay with me talking about how *our* college was funded by capitalist weapons producers, military whoevers. She said, "some people believe in defending our country and when you speak against that it makes them uncomfortable."

Uncomfortable, truth is like that. *Can't spell SAUSAGE without USA!* And she didn't write me a good recommendation either, bitch! She was so mad at me because she didn't care if her algorithms led to devastation or whatever, Iran Contra whatever, 9/11 whatever, post WW2 whatever, and I didn't even know I was calling her out when I was. I could have been in Einstein's department of uber-analysis of geometric space-time but this MAGA bitch was pissed that I called her out for being against brown people.

They are all against brown people, that old apex predator: the Northern European descended American White Male, followed closely by his female. And if you don't fucking believe me, let's start with the Crusades with Richard the fucking Lionheart, hop on over to serfdoms or Ireland, the entire fucking indigenous genocide in the Americas, cheers jolly-ho for the Trail of Tears, and the Jungle of child labor, indentured servants, 400,000 Africans land on our hearty shores ripe for the whip and the breeding. Let's get modern, the violent rape of South American countries for land passage by Rockefeller and Carnegie, our industrial heroes! Today, Big Pharma needed bigger profits so they cut research and quadrupled four times over the price of medicines Americans can't live without while dropping the price of Viagra. I haven't even mentioned the Military Industrial Complex, for profit prisons or land-fills or 59 billion animals killed for food last year.

Let's talk about serial killers. Let's talk about rapists. Let's talk about school shooters.

Or not. Wouldn't want the big guy to get *uncomfortable*.

Maybe it's not such a big surprise that everyone lost their guts. Maybe they've never thrown a punch.

✶✶✶✶✶✶✶✶✶✶

My stomach is sick with coffee and I have to shit. John doesn't have the guts to kill himself. He's all show. Shitshow. He's a walking total disaster. From first moment wailing on the ground about his scoutmaster to the night he came home telling me about how he titty fucked this woman and then screamed in her face about how fat she was and how she'd never be me and then showed up nearly black out drunk at my house after totally denigrating this girl to right now with this cold cup of Cafe Bustello he has never done anything right.

I wanted every other girl to be totally fucked over because I hated them in a way I wasn't able to hate myself. And yesterday three hours after the break up, when we're supposed to be living out the last few moments of our being forced to be together because rent and we're supposed to be figuring out how to not hurt each other and anyway he is just still trying to get his dick sucked. We're supposed to be figuring out how to break up peacefully and I walk in to him on the ground in front of the toilet taking sexy pictures about "layering up" and that means some bunny is asking him to stay warm and that's about more than just getting fingers stuck down your throat awkwardly and now I have to hate him again except this is what I expect from men. A lie, a total lie, he loves when you are sexually available and when you aren't, FUCK YOU.

He used the story about titty-fucking that fat girl in the back seat as a way to leverage me out of being poly. I was actually super happy being poly before that. But then I was with somebody really talented and with who there might have been a future, and when he saw that (because I told him, because that's what poly folks do) he had a spasmodicon eruption and went and Weinstein-ed some woman with a vengeance and realistically that's what he is also doing to this woman on the other side of the "layering up" photo. He's super into the pressurings he can justify, like how he sucked off his old best friend while he was sleeping and never stops claiming: *but we were ALWAYS making dick jokes!* Which as we all know in super-privileged-good-old-boy-cis-het-white-fuck language means *they were asking for it.* Nevermind he lost that friend and so many others, but John is innocent as peaches and puppies. Despite his lady clothes and lip stick he is still a rich boy misogynist. Fuck-ass.

This betty on the hook prolly has no idea about me or his ten personas or how I'm waiting for him to be dead today and chewing on the edges of my nails until they bleed. How my face is pressed into an impostor pillow I don't relate to. How I chastise myself about waiting on the other side of a silent door waiting to text his mom about the dead body. She doesn't even know his mom, or the trust fund, or his brother or how he is actually just leading her on about any kind of future. Or the lost friends, or the crying drunk in the night and how he moans *I just want my mom to love me.* Or how he sticks his tongue out and closes his eyes and covers his ears and goes *I'm not listening I'm not listening* when he doesn't want to hear/ see you and how he's not doing it ironically. She doesn't have the first idea what it's really like living with him day in and day out, the tension, the psychotic drinking, the threats, the never changing.

Victor Frankl wrote the essential treatise on this subject. If you haven't read him, I don't fucking care what you think. "When we are no longer able to change a situation, we are challenged to change ourselves." John is a spoiled brat, he's consummately unchallenged, self-centered and lazy disaster drinking himself stupid while he's waiting for his parents to croak so he can get his inheritance.

Still when I say disaster, I really mean just me.

Does the guy wearing the *I'm with Stupid* --> shirt really have anything to brag about?

No Dating:

I made home fries this morning in the oven on the cast iron skillet, and then forgot when I took them out about how hot the handle would be. I grabbed it with every confidence and now my hand is fucking burned. I'm soaking it in cool water as the internet tells me to do, and the pain is GD intense so I finish the whiskey. Now the trash has changed. I mark it in my memory for when I check later. The burn fucking hurts. It's just this kind of shit that happens when I'm busier thinking about that asshole in the next room than about my own GD life. Everything is quiet now which is no surprise since he's probably dead but also because he works nights and is used to sleeping all day.

I inventory the host of my other injuries: my pinky finger cuticle is torn to the first knuckle today, the rift is a french tip wide and the inner part is deep enough to be an open bleeder. Third finger right hand, too. Nobody notices the pus-crusty when I flick it off and start to chew again. Plasma, healing agent. Cut the damage out. My feet are frozen and more numb than the usual nerve damage and actually feel like just lead weights. The little safety glass cuts from the car windows bursting are barely noticeable across my cheek, shoulders and legs now. I don't turn the heat up past 52 degrees, just enough to keep the pipes from freezing. It's been below zero for 24 days straight and the Kaw River is frozen through, she's my sweetheart, soul mate, mirror, we both usually fast moving and tumultuous.

The Missouri River ice is cartwheeling and smashing mountains of slush against the rest of the floes at the confluence, but me and Kaw are both frozen still, my body is an igloo containing lost civilizations. My hand is burnt and buzzing with the cold of the water bath. My lips are an onslaught of gnashing teeth and I'm sucking blood hand to mouth, hand to mouth. The worst part of it though is that my dreams are coming out of their caskets again.

Every morning is an essay of investigating if what I remember really happened. Yes, Friday night he drove me home psycho drunk, fighting and then we broke up. I shake the thought of his cock in my mouth away. Yes, Saturday afternoon he asked me to help him take sexy pictures for some other woman, yes, his exact words were "Daddy's trying to get his swerve on." Yes that was the last time I saw him alive. Yes, I spoke to Dreya and I did not speak to Frannie. Yes, Saturday night I drank the whole bottle of whiskey, I have no memory of that. I have no memory of what I talked to Dreya about. I do remember Logan reached out to me on the Gram, but in the morning that wasn't real. I do remember pulling off my shoes and my toes all had frostbite, the little picky nubbin was already gone and the rest were like snot-twisted black Kleenexes. I check, that's not real. All pink and fine. Yes, Sunday night I came home and John is apparently in the bedroom and I promised myself I wouldn't check on him ever fucking again. No, Vegas did not burn to the ground. Yes, I left a stray hair on the toilet seat so that it would fall off when he lifted the lid to piss and I would know he was still alive. Yes, the hair is still there. Yes, the pain from the burn pulses in the same space a stigmata would be. And that's the inventory of all the pain there is today.

Nothing else at all.

I take the blue bowl of cold water for my burned hand into the front room to the couch and lay and watch the wind in the trees outside through the window. I like it when there are no leaves, because you can see all the opossum nests and squirrels and you can see so far. I turn the record on to Etta James.

I've given up on the pillows and now am just using the square cushion from the recliner chair. It's rough with 70's mustard weave and age and the edge just drops off which causes my neck to tilt and hang in air. Everybody has had it worse than me, any caring about bleeding on this couch is my vanity convincing itself it matters. That's what makes me so fucking pissed off about John. He has goose down and things called duvets, piques, plisses and matelasses. I call those blankets. He has a trust fund and when his dad bought him his new car, sure he pays him back, but each month's payment goes into a special high-interest yielding savings account for his future. So not only has John got wheels, he's got a retirement plan and he's got a suicidal tendency that keeps me locked to this couch in the living room because his Dad doesn't know the pain his son's in, only me. Dad just thinks his son is fucking worthless.

And he is. King of the Losers, Crown Prince of the Fuckarounds, Svengali of lost cause orphaned self-abusing wondershows. He's a Trashpeople and lined up two Trash Whores in the early hours of Saturday morning within thirty minutes of waking up single. I think Baton Rouge bitch's prolly some Anais rich in power +8 level mage witch with lace face tattoos who plays guitar and opens beer bottles with her teeth. What she probably is is a 56-year-old fake-titty silver-spoon bitch living off Daddy's credit card and pretending to be 32. Like it's totally worse to say you are 32 and look 52 than to be 56 and look 52. Whatever any of that shit means. She's got a 2011 Porsche Boxer and says she'll let him drive it 150 miles an hour through *their* suburbs. Yeah, their suburbs, because that's what they are. Products of products. Nobody's had an original thought for years. Everybody's terrified of the idea of an original idea because then they might not have a pat answer. And he'll call her "Sugar Momma." Fucking clichés.

I hate the suburbs. Tracts of houses, tracts of big box stores, an infinite array of streetlights and literally everywhere you look, just fucking instructions to obey: no left turn, green light, walk now, come on in we're open, pay before you pump, this way to the next set of gas station-food-lodge and they are all the same logo. We know a history of logos, when Walmart went brown, when Wal-Mart added the hyphen, so sophisticated! Hyphens. We're real readers here, put a hyphen in a black girl's name and all of a sudden she's unhirable. I hate fucking suburban parks, they are so manufactured. The squirrels don't run from a fucking dog because they've never met one off-leash before. A little pitty would rip out a heart a minute.

Also, all the flowers are neat in beds, all the trees are relieved of their wind-murdered limbs, all the grass is uniform and vivid, the kiddie pool is fucking fenced in already! And that's where most everybody is sitting, under a tent, at a metal table, feet solid on concrete, watching kids play in chlorinated water, contained by a 12-foot chain link fence, surrounded by manicured grass and trees guaranteed to be free of oak mites, with comfortable parking, security cameras, a sunset curfew, police presence, no alcohol allowed, guns fine, safety concrete on the playground and a NO DOGS OFF LEASH sign. And about a thousand other signs, too. What's suburban life without an instruction manual of metal signs on posts? They're great readers, literate, every GD one.

John and Sugar Momma don't know what's underneath rocks, don't know how to read the spring of the trees, don't notice the asshole suburban squirrels, would scream if they saw a snake in all that *civilization*, in fact they wouldn't even go there and neither would I so what am I going on about with daydreaming about them somewhere like the sunlight. They'll be in a dive bar buying rounds of shots for the nearest 10 people because the only way they know of making friends is through showing off a fat fucking wad. Thanks, Dad!

But they'll pretend to be self-made. Because it's not *cool* to live off mom and dad. Hey, fuck-asses! Guess what? That's the surest sign to us *actually* poor motherfuckers that you are rich. We're all jealous as fuck, we're all wondering what we'd be with the chances you had, we're all wishing we had somebody to call to bail us out or pick us up from the bus station. It hasn't occurred to us that savings accounts even exist, we don't know there is such a thing as a financial planner, much less that that person would call our parents if we missed a yearly consulting session. We daydream of hopping trains and setting off for the Amazon river basin from Kansas City in our kayaks. We kinda think we might make it just on being real and having a dream. I prolly have uterine cancer but can't afford to know and even if I could, there's no one to take care of me if I was sick.

There's no fucking reason for me to be dwelling on all this. It's a waste of my fucking time. Maybe if I just get my head comfortable I can nap for a couple hours then maybe I can leave. My hand hurts, my mouth hurts, my head hurts, I can't cry. All the salt and water is just trapped inside me.

✳✳✳✳✳✳✳✳✳✳

I flip the pillow to see if there is any familiarity. There's not. The room is too dark so I go rip off the black plastic from my front room window and expose the slatted blinds. There's nothing to see here, folks. Just the *toots and pedos.* That's prostitutes and pedestrians, which-is-which is a fun game to play. Most people are all *path of least resistance* and that's like totally normal, whole realms of physics describe this phenomenon, they're called Lagrangians and it's its whole own reference frame where you kinda make that assumption and then all these complex dynamics are just a pretty straight line, easy-peasy-on-your-kneesy. And it's not even fair to be like *they're lazy* or *they lack imagination* or *they're self-harming* because it's really not that complex. It's just dangerous to deviate from the norm, the equations don't work anymore, your fingernails bleed, you're outside acceptable margins, your pillow gets replaced, your teeth are crooked … or they are straight and white and that means clean and rich. Ya hear me? Who wouldn't want that?

This bitch on the street corner gonna keep suckin dick for her whole life, and she's got a couple regulars including the pancho in the green house, and they prolly treat her nice and know her name and everything. Hell they've prolly paid her rent and for an abortion once or twice. Is she fulfilled? Nah, but she got ramen and a landlord who doesn't rape her and for all she knows that's peace. And maybe it fucking is. Have I really got so much better with this gutter-infatuated frat boy with ten personalities and he can't tell the difference between a one of em and the only thing they all have in common is whiskey. He comfortable there too and anyways always got that safety net of mommy and daddy.

My momma kicked it three years ago. My dad's long dead. John's my safety net and you can add that up three ways to Sunday and it equals nothing but I don't know if he's dead or not in the bed but I'm not gonna open that door, like ever.

If he's takin the easy way out then so am I.

Our romance was never *deep* or *complicated*, anyway. The first time John and I drank together was when we knew we had something rare, though. Both of us were just so *spontaneous* and *self-destructive*. Yeah, we knew we were damaged goods and we didn't give a fuck. Our whole game was to get kicked out of places as fast as possible. He's 6'5" in four inch wedge heels, hot pink fishnets and a deep v cut big black and white print, he has the GG Alin leather with the chain. I'm in white skinny jeans, a tattered bra and my oxbloods with the Tyler Durden red leather and oversize orange shades. We walk into Dave's and *boom!* Instantly kicked out, John's made plenty of enemies everywhere.

Westport is a kick in the balls, it's so fucking bleak nothing we do gets any real attention. We're at Buzzard and we're beating the shit out of each other on the patio, I'm just climbing up his tall ass lanky and trying to pull him down to the ground and he's trying to throw me over his shoulder. We're falling into tables and we're feng-shui-ing the room with our bodies' anthem to sledgehammers. We push through the crowds and back towards the bar, all doing this panther cuddling routine we've worked up. I know this is part of what he misses about me now, but god-damn, I'm not into doing the same shit over and over forever, shit's got GD seasons.

But here we are blocking the front door and the bathrooms both and I've got him to the fucking floor already and now I'm kicking his back as hard as I can with my docs on and he's just sorta full on punching me in the cunt. All of a sudden I'm cuffed and hauled sky-high and eye-to-eye with the big-ass bouncer, Panda. I'm just a rotating side of beef on his meat-cleaver of an arm. John, too.

"I know you two are just having fun, but to everyone else it looks like I'm allowing a domestic assault to happen." Panda growls at us with a jealous grin and throws us out with a swish of his hand that very clearly states *not tonight, bitches*. Everybody eating at rock bottom bar wants a piece of this abandon, and that's even how we think of it:

once I was abandoned, now I have abandon.

We were out to cure our pasts by re-inflicting everything that had been done to us on each other, and then the pain would be ours. Mine. Then the pain would come from someone you really loved instead of the fucks who let us down and didn't ever really know us. And it worked.

For a while.

Then all our bridges were burned, and nobody ever stuck their head out for me again and maybe nobody ever had to because I was just born tougher than the rest. Blah-blah-blah childhood trauma this, neglect that, this rape that rape, just shit didn't matter to me as much as getting the fuck away from it so that's what I did. But I'm lying if I'm saying that nobody giving me a half-ass chance isn't prolly part of why I give everyone else so many chances. I'm always feeling like you can never tell what's on the other side of true comradery, what's on the other side of real family, what it would be like if nobody gave up on nothing and everybody fought instead. Frankl said *those who live are those who feel like there's something to live for* and that's what I'm doing. I'm living on the chance of future and the past is a shithole so fuck that. I'm a futurist.

Today I'm gonna get off of this couch and I'm not going to see if he's dead in there because he's allowed to die if he wants to. We both know we can never have the night back where he drank my piss from a plastic cup in a bar on the Plaza and then poured the last drops down the back of the woman hitting on him and swept me up in a drooling kiss. He just pours saliva out of his mouth-breathing face. He spits on you with every rampaging tirade against *calming down* all while he's legally parked. His ears stink of dead flesh constantly because of flophouse-stretched gauges. You can smell him a foot away. He's always doing that pressurized nasal cavity slurp of snot down the back of his throat. His nose hairs only emerge out of the top, inner part of nostrils you could fit a full-sized Bic lighter into and there is inevitably a booger hanging off of them. But he meticulously shaves every other hair on his body to a smooth gonna-be-stubble again in less than two hours. Everywhere you touch him it's a thousand small dull needles.

We'll never get kicked out of bars again the same way we did when we were just kids. Everything's gone too far and now I have to learn how to give up on something I love. I have to know I'll never be able to tell the story of what happened after he drank my warm salty piss again, because there's no one but him who'd understand.

But I gotta listen to Sharon, and she told me, "You can't love a man more than he loves himself, he'll just drag you down with him."

And we're all drowning in this house, it's the easiest way to get there.

✷✷✷✷✷✷✷✷✷✷

Potato Eater fingers. So gross. The only reason we know Vincent van Gogh's work now is because after his bastard brother died and left a broke-ass bitch (nothing's really changed since the Industrial Revolution) is because the sister-in-law widow was like, "all I got is these shithole Vincent paintings, but damned if there aren't a lot of them." And she didn't just make a fortune, she made a fortune for a fuck-ton of folks who made White Iris and Crows over a Wheatfield posters, coffeemugs, notebooks, calendars, checkbooks, mouse pads. Remember mouse pads? Ha. Anyway, she fed her kids and now old white dudes can make millions of dollars and we peasants have our Patron Saint, van Gogh.

What did Mike Tyson say to van Gogh? *You gonna eat that?*

When I was sucking my first boyfriend's dick, I didn't know what cum was, and I felt his shaft *undulate* and then spurt my mouth full of slimy, backwater tartar sauce QUITE unexpectedly. Yah, I gagged. I did not eat *that* or swallow, just made a GD fool of myself on a park bench scraping the taste out of my mouth with my fingernails.

After Gary touched my asshole he sucked his fingers while he thought I was asleep.

There's a ragged edge on my thumbnail I've been picking at all morning.

John's anorexic and I eat his hidden, stale cookies.

My aunt told my cousins in front of me about how they'd never be as smart as me. I was 9.

I have a deep cut on the back of my right hand just below the thumb that I don't know how I got because I was too blotto and I keep picking it open and I secretly hope I can keep it open forever.

The ring fingernail of my right hand is swollen with infection.

The pus bubble on the inside of my palm burst and is a flaming dagger of pain.

John's face is burned because last week he started a trash fire in the back yard and "accidentally" threw two spray paint cans in it. One blew up right in his fucking face and I turned around from getting another warm beer from the paper bag to see the junkie on fucking fire, like legit viral youtube video on fucking fire from the tip of his right hand up his arm, over his chest and all over his fucking face. I yelled "STOP DROP AND ROLL!" But he didn't, he just ran away and luckily the fumes went out quickly and his face is crispy bacon and his hand is swollen like a red skin glove full of fucking pus.

He started a kickstarter called "Got Fired, Caught Fire" and scammed $450 bucks in less than two hours off saps who care about him. He wasn't fired from his job, he was suspended for workplace violence against a woman I might add. He did catch fire but it's because he threw spray paint cans in a GD fire he started. It's whatever, this money guarantees that he's gonna fucking leave this house and me forever, but that's also exactly why I don't understand why the fuck he isn't already gone. I know for a fact he's got two g's in savings and another $800 in the bank and two rich parents who'll float him forever, so what's the fucking hold up, Dummy?

Chad's breath smelled like burned macaroni and a gallon of mayonnaise spilled on the floor.

My cheeks are raw from biting.

Neither of us are managing to eat a thing. Nothing has moved in the kitchen or any of the three trash cans. We gotta feed a fever and starve a cold but both of us are made of ice.

My toes are not frost bitten and what happens at home stays at home, just like Vegas.

My clit is still hurt from failing at masturbating too hard.

If you are dead set on making some man *yours* I got just one thing to say to you: go into his computer, look at his saved porn (if you're lucky he'll be a real fetishist) or if you can't find it, search his history for what he's watching. Check it out and take notes. These are the sex acts you do, *oh coy!* You know how. This is what it is for John: topless, unshaved pits, one arm up over the head and smoking, leaning against a wall holding a bottle (like a handle) of rot gut whiskey and wearing sunglasses, a gap tooth or else those weird extra canines, really just anything screwy with your teeth. If your teeth look like a brawl at a Black Friday Sale, he wants to fuck you. He likes that because it's a guarantee you are poor and he fetishizes poor people and orphans. No rich people have funky teeth.

I'm poor, but my teeth are fine. Blessed with the good genes and good too because the number one correlation with getting real old is having all your original teeth. I plan on outliving fucking everyone. And now you're all *I don't wanna be infirm or in pain or not able to take care of myself.* Fuck you to death then, go get your death and breathe it in, wallow around in your resignation, yunno that terrible old people smell. You are already infirm and in pain and co-dependent and lost and you don't know nothin about nothin and if you don't wanna live then I got better things to do than fuck with you.

So one night I buy this R&R plastic pint and pall-mall unfiltereds and I'm always half naked anyway so that part comes naturally. I lean into his doorstep with that cigarette hanging and exhale just as he opens the door. Right into his face. Men like to be denigrated. It's this whole complex thing. They don't realize their most vulnerable point is actually their hard prick: they think that's what makes them strongest and that's actually why women will always have the power.

Sharon tells a story of this quick-thinking woman friend who woke up to a rapist knifing off her clothes, and she just starts caterwauling all banshee-whore style with *yeah, baby give it to me, fuck me good little boy, mamma been waiting for your hard hard dick* and damned if his pinger didn't go all softee-waftee and he runs crying from the room.

Same way they like a little humiliation, I think of it as their subconscious secretly desiring equality. So he grins through the smoke and lets me in and I immediately take off the white wife-beater. (Gotta wonder how that gem became a thing.) My tits don't drop so good because they're pert but the nipples are just perfect. Definite high point, real pink and goldilocks just right. He physically licks his lips. I take a slog of the whiskey and pass it over to him. Stub the cigarette out into his floor. You know what happened after that.

I mean, he wrote me love letters after that! Once he showed up at 11 am, near black out drunk on my porch with a six foot fancy yard flower all broken stem in the middle where his toddler-fist crushed it and roots still clumped with dirt. I'm sitting out there smoking and he falls to the ground and hand digs a hole into the janky flower garden creepy-neighbor sorta tends and plants this son-of-a-bitch. I mean, that's romantic.

Searching the porn out serves two purposes: one, he's sunk into your pussy magic and two, you know how to trip his trigger so good that the whole sex part can just get the fuck over with already.

✶✶✶✶✶✶✶✶✶✶

I know he's gonna come out of there sometime today. I mean he's not above pissing in a bottle, but he will definitely not shit the bed, I mean it's against the rules. He's gonna come to his senses and climb into the couch next to me and I'll forget about the pillow and we'll go to the Denny's by his work and he'll tell me about the wheel size on Toyota Tacomas and what's happening on late night AM radio. I know he'll come back around.

Whatever if I'm a real Know-It-All-Nelly, I don't feel like I should feel bad about that. Actually, I don't think people should feel bad about most things like really 99% or better of things. We're just conditioned to feel bad because somewhere we picked up this ERMERGD meme along the line when someone we like is watching and so now that's what's good, Miley. Fuck all that. So it pisses me off when I don't know something and even though I ain't shit and I was fucking robbed of my intellectual birthright I still manage to read a fuck ton and learn a shithole and listen, right. Ya'll like to call me *la tiburona* and all that but at the same time each of you has admitted more *to me* than you have prolly to anyone else in your entire life. Yeah, so shit's complex, and I've always been like *yo! everybody get yours.*

So I don't give a fuck about all the things and I just want a house boat and a hound dog. A horizon. The Mexicans say about the Pacific that it doesn't have a memory. I want that ocean. My mind's all fucked up because I've been living with a dysfunctional alcoholic or another for my entire life. My mind's all fucked up because I'm so desperate to get out and I've been spinning my wheels, and Jonah didn't get out and Delilah didn't get out and Persephone didn't get out and Maya didn't get out and Carl didn't get out.

Why can't dinosaurs clap? *Because they're dead.*

And if one more person says "o but if I had to do it all over again, I'd do it just the same because I just *love* who I am now." Fuck that so hard. Fuck who I am now, hurting people all over the place and not meaning to, black out drunk and fucking everybody up and me too. Me fucking too and I mean that both ways. I know exactly the moment I would go back and change. I know six or seven of them actually, depending on where's reasonable to turn back time and re-fucking-start.

So nobody loves a know-it-all more than me. I just wanna be the dumbest person in the room for a minute. That's why I keep going to that open mic to see Sharon. Sharon's old and don't get listened to much and that's to the deficit of the entire world because if Jesus GD Crucifix is on this planet he's in the form of this too old, regular sized, hawk nosed, biker mama who carries her own water and aint never been nothin but nonplussed. She says to me: "Best get what you want, cuz there's no tellin what anybody else actually wants. Then least somebody get theirs." GD right old gal. I never been spirit-fucked better than by Sharon, this old bitch given me more than 1000 books could, and with a Jack Nicholson grin and a pep in her old ass step. She knows the deep tap root of pain and her name is woman.

Last month I go see Mama Shiva Sharon and she sings a song about how all she got from her *dear old dad* is this *shit eatin grin*. She tells a story about being hard-packed-dirt poor and following her Daddy everywhere she could which wasn't much being as he wasn't much home. How she looked up to him and how he never spoke to her. She followed him out the back door one day onto the parched deep landscape of loss, no grass, no wheat, no money, no tenderness. He pulled out his cock and pissed in the dirt. Sharon says how in awe she was of how powerful the force of his water, the sound filling her ears and raising the dust of the hard dirt as the liquid swelled the land and went running off downhill. So she decides she's gonna do the same thing, and pulls down her pants, arching her little back into the wind and pushes hard. She does not gush, she tinkles, the urine running down her legs and into her socks. This little girl turns to face her father as he puts himself away. He looks at her and says

"God damn worthless little girl, can't even piss hard on the ground right."

Sharon chuckles and goes into the chorus of her song again, she's laughin about that *shit eating grin.* We all know it's been nothing but a pissing contest this whole time. I all of a sudden am the proud parent of an entire ocean of peacefulness. She lights up a big cigar and winks at me. I like to be winked at. This is the magic of a real mother, every burden they see as pleasure, every lesson they take pleasure in teaching: here's how you go to kindergarten, here's how you listen to music, how you change your oil, here's how you define infinity, here's how you know you exist, eyes are input devices, not output devices. Here's how you know what you see exists only within you. Here's how you piss yourself.

Here's me saying I wish I'd listened to you better, old lady.

I hear your raspy voice whispering in my ear:

> been rode hard and put away wet
> aint been broke yet

And I want to be you. Maybe I pretend to be you for a little while today and I can figure out a way to leave this catastrophe. Or maybe he'll come out of the bedroom to take a shit.

✶✶✶✶✶✶✶✶✶

The afternoon drags on and I try to doodle a little, and I try to sweep the floors silently and I research Hieronymus Bosch a bit and I can't help but wonder what that guy's fucking deal was. That guy's got baggage, he's definitely damaged goods. I wish I was fucking him instead of the junkie. The first time John and I broke up was because he lied to me about shooting dope and he lied to me about being tested for HIV. Just lied right to my GD face. After bragging about the French Bitch and how it was ok to rape her because she was a whore and owed him rent money. The second time we broke up was because he told me that his ultimate dream was not just to kill himself, but to also kill everyone who'd ever loved or hated him in a grand spree, because the only way to truly die was to kill yourself and to also kill the memory of yourself and that's how he wanted to go. He called it *having duende* after some Spanish bastard. To him, nothing is better than being a Spaniard.

He tried to explain to me A LOT how it was so romantic and meant he was a real artist, and I was just like *no motherfucker, you are literally threatening to kill me.* And to this fucking day he stands by his word that killing me would be a good thing and that I'm some kind of suck-ass for not being real magical Spanish enough to get it. Prolly he just wants me to sacrifice myself for him or wants to feel like he owns my life, or that he could sneak those hands around my neck and call it romance. And what's fucked up more than that? I let him sleep next to me again. I let him put his cock in me again. I let him anything me again.

And trust me, it's not that I didn't yell at him. I fucking yell at him so much it sounds like nothing more than the trains we're used to living next to, the mice in the kitchen with their incessant scratching, the peeling skin of a second degree burn, all the things we can't fucking get rid of. I yell at him about how I won't have a scale in my house and there won't be any weigh-ins, about how he needs to use clean needles if he's gonna nod out with Quick, about doing the dishes and how fucking Thursday is trash day and how all I want is that if he's gonna go around saying he's some fab-o fantastico psycho shitstorm than at least he should fucking write poems, do any-fucking-thing.

Because there's the rub, he just says he's an artist, and he totally looks like one, and acts like an asshole and that's how folks expect *superior* people like artists to act, but the truth in the dark alley is not a $10 hand job, but it's a limp dick in his own hand and the stench of a dumpster. He's impotent as fuck when it comes to literally lifting his pen even though he can fuck for days and come like 6-7 times a day at minimum. If semen was a chapbook he'd be motherfuckin prolific as Hector GD Martinez, and published everywhere. But actually he's just a limp ass little troll who don't pen a GD thing, but critiques it ALL.

Oh he could raise a red flag or two with how much he pretends to know. And I yell at him until I'm raw in the throat and he just *dissociates* away and I'm no more than a cricket dripping out of a faucet on the third floor guest bathroom of his childhood home. And what's he gotta listen to me for anyway? What have I got to give that his fancy-ass family can't?

His best friend came over one time and they were like laughing and having so much fun and Eli works in LA and gets snacks for dudes who star in Netflix shows and Eli's going on and on to John about how in LA (John interrupts and says *as I like to say HELL-A* like he's fucking clever or something) and they both laugh more and Eli goes on to talk about how fucking poor they both are compared to what happens in The Valley and the people he knows live *actually* large.

The laugh I gave them was so epically snide both their dicks hid and they shut their eyes and looked at me for a story. I just glared at John and said, "Why don't you tell Eli about the first time you saw the house I grew up in?"

The truth is the house was small but in my memory it had been a mansion. It was so big my little sister once left a cereal bowl in a back room so long that when we found it the milk had turned to a bowl full of maggots. It had a separate two car garage like in the movies. There were two floors and a staircase. And when John stood in front of the house I was embarrassed to not understand basic proportions.

The truth is the fences were so tall because we could double our income twice a year with the price on the coonhound puppies. This is how we fed ourselves. In my memory every puppy was my friend and John hadn't even seen the back field, the creek or the walking bridge yet so how could he fucking even know what it was like to grow up here? But I saw what he saw too and that shack was a dirty fucking shithole and that is where I was from. I'd seen where he was from and his room was so nice his mother wouldn't even let him stay in it, true fucking story. John lived in the concrete floored basement.

"So I just fell to my knees and literally cried. Like burst into tears because not only is this where she's from, people still fucking live there!" John exclaims and he and Eli are laughing harder than ever.

I can hear those echoes in this house, the house that John and I share and that his mother doesn't know about. My eyes see the afternoon light and it's because the sun is up and the blinds won't reach to the bottom of the windowsill and I'm stuck on the couch which is in the front room and so the sunshine is infesting my eyes and right now I'm wide awake even though I desperately want to sleep. I should have left the black plastic up. It's so fucking cold in here. I fold the doodle of John's decapitated body and put it underneath the empty whiskey bottle. I wonder if he's got more in there.

I pull the duvet John's mom bought him up and over my eyes but around my nose so I can still breathe. I want to go back to sleep. I want to sleep forever and ever and ever like if Sleeping Beauty never woke up that'd be me. Seriously, what's she got to get after "Prince Charming" wakes her up? A lifetime of shut-the-fuck-up and I-wish-you-were-dead and pissy-bitch-fuck. No thank you. I turn into the couch and close my eyes like a salvation.

Jesus died for somebody's sins but not mine.

My cheek meat is sore and my fingers hurt and my feet are cold and I'm hungry even though I'm not an anorexic so I'm allowed to eat but I just want to sleep some more but I can't sleep. And now I'm awake and I have to listen for John in the next room. *Shhhhhhhh.*

I hold my ear out to the cold. Everything is so so silent. I can't hear youtube, or snoring, or texting *bloops* or masturbating. I can't hear anything and it's like the beginning of the world. Suddenly everything is possible. Suddenly, I'm not so sure anymore if I really care if he's dead or alive or if that's all just a habitual behavior of wifedom and womanhood. I feel a lightness in the quiet.

Maybe I'm not as much of a woman as I thought.

Maybe if he's dead it doesn't actually matter to anyone at all.

✶✶✶✶✶✶✶✶✶

I don't know how I got to be sucking his dick when the house was burning to the ground. He slides his body on top of mine and comes before he can stick it in, replete with embarrassment and mess. He's back, he's here. The burning house somehow doesn't matter, and I have this idea that it wasn't ours anyway but I did go back in after he came too fast and grabbed our computers. It doesn't make sense about the extra rooms in the basement and the dirty kids fucking around there but then I woke up with slatted evening light caging my face and this is the prison I made and here I am alone on the couch. The pillow feels funny. I turn it over and over to check for signs of tampering. What really happened when I was asleep? Did he leave?

I check myself. I have all my clothes on and the house hasn't actually burned down so now I know I didn't actually suck his dick and that means I still don't know the yes or no of him in that room because you don't know if the cat is alive or if the cat is dead until you open the box and I haven't done that and right now, nothing could make me even though my heart is beating a thousand thumps a minute and it's because I'm afraid he's gone. I can't move one inch. I'm the not-looking immovable object against the what-if-he's-gone unstoppable force. I'm a frozen to death flightless bird. Sharon once told me the story of a hundred and two year old woman who she spent nights with when the family couldn't afford the overnight nurse. Tabitha was the architecture of degenerative bone disease and also couldn't leave her bed. Sharon stayed up nights with the lace skinned woman because when you are that close sleeping is furtive.

Maybe I'm closer than I know. But in the night there are whispers and stories arrive unbeckoned and sometimes one needs to find peace by relenting the last of the shame and rage away and that's not what is happening here but it might have been what was happening there. Sharon is a box cutter and she opened Tabitha up. The now-gone girl told a story of how her father would come to her palette in the night when she was undeveloped and ask to see. The girl would lift her shift over the spare shoulders of a peasant, daughter of a bee-keeper, a well-digger, an olive-harvester, a seasonal worker and she would get worked over and sown by her father in the night.

He pinched her nipples and complimented when they twisted taut. He said, "I can't wait until you get your hairs" and lift her arms and spread her legs and investigate her the way he would assess the burrow's hooves or the dog's teeth or the day's take from the boss. Tabitha never mentioned falling asleep after. He got caught in the act one day though and the mother and the aunt made sure they found a way to send Tabitha off to an uncle in America and that's how a pre-pubescent good girl came to make a life in America as a woman and she'd never told a soul about her father's touches except Sharon in the fading of her time.

Sharon looks at me, and says "Tabitha told me she'd never told another soul about that, and then she looked away from me and said: *he never did get to see my breasts.*"

I know just how she feels.

There's something about wanting to please a man and be loved by him. There's something about doing anything he asks of you. No matter how abusive and careless and cheating he is, we just see some potential in him. We think we know him better than everyone else. We think getting his love makes us special. We think we are being patient and kind. Well, you can call it duty or compassion or whatever but really you are just a fucking doormat. You still want him to like your servitude, even you'll be that instead of yourself just to keep him around. There's a day hoping to darken around me and I can taste the water rising and I'm salty af. There's gonna come a retribution for all of us.

There's gonna come a come-uppance and these GD men calling themselves fathers or lovers are gonna get fucking cracked like that burning house. Of course the house is burning to the ground, all the men who fucking built it are fucking over all the women who fill it with life. Never met a woman who hasn't been raped. Sometimes they don't even know it themselves yet, they think they are blessed and god watches over them and I wish I knew what it took to be blessed in this world but I was born bad. Some alien architecture building my stratosphere of impossible and futile dreams and left with nothing but nightmares. Fuck god. Fuck Jesus even. Jesus died for somebody's sins but not Tabitha's father's. Or Sharon's father's, or mine, or for fucking John, who was born with it all and then just fucking pissed it away.

I miss my mom suddenly but she never even noticed what was happening and anyway there's no safe uncle in America, we're not in Vegas we can't just keep keeping silent, the pillow is changing colors and size, van Gogh will never see a dollar, I have a cut on the back of my hand that won't heal a dry cunt a cut hood my eyes are bench pressing Olympic weights placing wrinkles arriving over furrowed brows. Worry lines, frown lines from where my face was pushed down into the ashy floor, held down while I was jack-rabbitted, holding my breath while my step-father held a threatening fist, and that's why I'm dissociating into the wide expanse of ocean and returning to the salt and water where the only fire is the distant sun and I'm gone gone gone.

If there are any houses burning to the ground, it's because John left a cigarette burning after he passed out jerking off.

✶✶✶✶✶✶✶✶✶✶

I can hear the bluetooth speaker making the text noises. He's moved from Tinder to texting I know. He's alive. And dating. Three fucking days after we break up and he's already got at least two women who are either willing to fuck a dude who is still married and living with his wife or else he's a liar. How desperate is everyone?

Dating is a complete waste of time, either be the fuck in love or fuck off, or be friends or whatever, but as the saying goes *nobody wants to talk to someone they can't fuck.* I did my share of fucking before I met John and he wrangled me into being monogamous. After my one big relationship with Darryl was "Little Fish" obviously he went to Burning Man, and after him was Sarah and she couldn't stop smoking meth, it's Missouri after all, and then Trevor with the shaved head who killed himself later and then the dirty kid on the mattress in the abandoned building and others I don't think of at night anymore and then Frannie but we were just friends and then John. Course none of that counts Gary or Chad.

I'm into three ways and light choking, not like with my scarf though, and anal. I hate blow jobs but pretend not to, of course, otherwise he'll never cum and you'll be down there all day. Anal sex is ok in some ways, too. First of all, a butt-gasm is a real thing, like suddenly his cock is deep in your intestines and he's thrusting away and it must be sosososo tight and *impermissible* and he comes. so. quick. And then we're done, y'all and he's all king-of-the-world and everytime John stuck it up my ass in two years he sang a song about it for days after that went "I-*iiiiiii* got *buuuuuttttt-sex!!!*" But with like a throat singing at maximum pleasure and his actually beautiful voice trimoloing and ringing out and this like total pure joy. So yeah I gave it up to him and sometimes it was ok.

The first time though, he shoved it in and I jumped up, mad as hell, pulled my drawers up and ran in the pissing rain for ¾'s of a mile down Valentine past the park towards the hospital. I didn't know where I was going. But there I was at Bell and 38th and embarrassed and just walked on back over and there the junkie is watching "Hobo with a Shotgun" and we snuggled. He doesn't ever call me out on my shit. He's just happy I'm back.

Anal sex is also A+ because #NOBABIES and babies are a drag. And yunno there's this thing about making someone completely happy/thrilled/whatever. And when I let him fuck me up the butt, it feels like that, like I really matter and we'll be together forever and I'd have a family and he'd love me for the pleasure and.

And.

And then I could be myself finally. I could trust somebody and they'd be there and John always said and still says he'll be family after the break up but I asked him "how many people from your past do you really talk to?"

He had to admit there were none.

John and Frannie hate each other. "Cock tease" he would say. "Trashperson" she would say. They were both right. Both are right. Although true story, last year it was her birthday and she wouldn't answer the phone and so I left a voicemail saying I would tattoo her name on John's ass if she didn't call me back, and she texted back that all she ever wanted for her birthday was her name tattooed on someone and that now we had to do it. So now John's ass is tattooed with the name of a woman he hates. So now he's just like every other shithole cunt sucker. Frannie was my best friend, she totally saved me from Darryl. Yeah he and me moved in together after he dropped out and I don't wanna think about the things that happened in that house but one day she just showed up on my doorstep and took charge.

I was lying in the bed with a razor blade on the bed stand and my suicide buddy's phone was turned off that day, fucking naturally, and I was close, man. And here's pigeon-toed Frannie in green docs and burgundy knee-highs over navy tights and stone-washed high-waisted jean shorts and a cut up *Y La Bamba* shirt, ear gauges big as the bottom of a tall boy and this wild ass undyed freestyle mohawk of brown hair. She just comes in my house all no-cares-in-the-fucking-world and is like, "pack, bitch."

We packed faster than I could imagine. A bitch with a mission is an unstoppable force. We've got the everything in the back of her pick-up, everything except my plants which of course he killed, and off we went. She took me to Beer Kitchen and we ate chicken and waffles and had powdered donut holes and lemon cream pie. Every time we go out to eat, she orders two desserts. It looks like one for me and one for her but really I only drink. Nowadays I know how all that sugar got returned to the earth. I know the secret of the locked bathroom door, but then, I just thought I was making her happy.

She looked at me, smug, right. She said, "you're not a fucking social worker. It's not your job to fix anyone."

I was never really trying to fix anyone, she had me dead wrong on that, that was her thing. No one was ever good enough for her, but I just liked people warts and all, or picking face anxiety and anorexia and all or whatever hodgepodge of grotesqueries whoever has. I never thought anyone was perfect. But I have always wanted an artist. Someone I can sink my teeth into, someone who isn't fucking boring.

Fuck dating. I'll take banging myself any day over that tire kicking. Gruel is my art. You know what that is? It's the wasted cum from masturbating. It's the thick spit on the ipad screen after letting that titty-drop gif play on infinite loop. It's the peek of a bitten lip in a dusty shadow and *skeet skeet skeet* right on her face. I like it when people send me photos of their cum on my naked pics. I'm everything they need, I'm a purveyor of pleasure without it having to take one ounce of my effort or skill, it's their imagination that is on fire, and when they send gruel pics and tell me their fantasies I'm living a thousand futures, each of which I'm a pure center of. For that one pop anyway.

And really, what do I need a real life man for anyway? I've always been imaginative, he may titty-fuck red-heads in back seats but I'm at home stitching my broken soul into an open wound. I'm over here with ten Boschian lovers and filled up in every hole, every pore, quaking with a palpable pleasure of pure battle. I know it's good when I'm climaxing with bated breath and my cunt grips the waves of my gruel and the tears of release are streaming down my peached cheeks and the salt left on my face tells exactly the story of how my heart broke when he fell in love with another woman 30-minutes to 3-hours after we broke up last Friday night.

I start to touch myself but can only see the two of them fucking and in my mind's eye she's is so much sexier than I am. I wish I was more than just a warm hole, and that he'd come out here and fuck me.

✶✶✶✶✶✶✶✶✶✶

I don't expect him to come out tonight, he's not the type that needs emotional support and if he stops to think about it, he'll know I don't want to hear about his climbing the "penis ladder" or "sugar mommas" and so he just won't come out. He might though. He did do nice things for me when we were together and I'm irreverently sad this is all coming to an end. And I guess all this means I think he's alive in there and if he's alive in there then he's avoiding me the same way I'm avoiding him, but he definitely doesn't think I might be dead even if he might be thinking of killing me. He's alive and he's gonna go on with his life.

John gave me a book of coupons a couple weeks after the first time we fucked, which was awful by the way, despite knowing his trips and triggers, because what I didn't know then was that all small-dicked mother-fuckers are super-outta-this-world insecure about their tiny pingers. I find most of them also have a cuckold fetish and I like to believe this is their subconscious really really wanting to please women. He has the hand-writing and spelling skills of a toddler despite the much touted *Jesuit Education*. The little "Guest Check" book lifted from the diner is labeled "CUPONS".

1 free fresh pair of wings

One free use of the name "Sparkle Princess"

One free opportunity to finally realize why I don't dance/ laughing at me as I try & dance

One free evening of me getting you high listening to Against Me! knitting, decoupaging & making useless things from wood, string, used toilet paper superglue & beer cans

One free "blood, poems, beers & queers"

1 free scoop

~~Two~~ One free Diner delivered – no Café Sebastin

One free middle of the night phone call – topic of your choice, all about you

One free push on the swings

One free Pony Prance to town & back

One free giggle untill you pee a little

One free coffee delivery "zoom zoom"

One free hour of being read to, so you can do other things, & not have to put your story down

One case of amnesia

One free fix from broken

Today I'm turning in those last two CUPONS because now we are the monsters and that wasn't how it was supposed to go, and if I can't ever not be a monster then that means I have to face that that's what I am. He can forget about me altogether and I can forget about him and we can be fixed from being broken and I won't have to hold my breath anymore while he's in the bedroom drinking whiskey/cokes mixed with wine and 5 hour energy drinks from the 2 liter bottle while singing at the top of his lungs about "I want a lover I don't have to love."

Sometimes ya just have to give a motherfucker what they ask for.

✶✶✶✶✶✶✶✶✶✶

This pattern of hiding in my house from men who are supposed to be family is becoming clear to me. When mom's husband Gary put his patriarchy there, with his finger, I went to my mom with a mouth full of bubble gum and casually demanded I no longer have a first floor bedroom and that the basement be totally remodeled and I must say with a private bath and closet and room all closeted within a locked door suite to which I had the only key. And now seriously, when a 12-year-old kid makes such specific demands, arrives with a rider to the second half of sixth grade, what kind of mother is like, *heywowcool and def you can have that, whee-hee-wowo!* Fucking cunt. Sure she didn't see. But I can't be that mad because first of all, imagine how bad their fucking was when he just wanted to stick a forefinger up the butt of little girls and she's like 500 years old compared to the Lolita of blowing out a dozen candles. It sucks to feel old. Womanhood is erased or reliquated to motherhood in the pop-culture mayhem of every decade's youth worship. Then Darryl, hiding from him drunkenly punching walls, but that's really just shit you deal with with any man. Trevor, rest his damned soul. Now this front room hide-out where I've covered the arching entry ways with patterned tapestries from the hippie shop on Broadway.

But if every story has a happy ending, then here's mine: I never told anybody what Gary did to me until Melanie was talking to me on the phone and I was caterwauling about how Gary was trying to control my life. It was high school and before my mom died and she was his wife and he felt like as a man he should have a say in how to deal with what a total shit-show I was. And Mel was my first girlfriend and as I was crying to her about how unfair my parents were I slipped and said "on top of everything else he molested me and so I should be the one with the power here, not fucking him."

And I hadn't told anyone before that. And it slipped out, and Mel said, "He's upstairs watching TV now right? Go up there and tell him to leave you alone. And tell him why."

I did just that. I walked out my private teenage suite, through the laundry room, past the puzzle table, up the garage stairs, in through the kitchen door, round past the dining room table and into the front room with lace curtains, blue carpet, beige walls and a woven striped couch and he was in a powder blue lounger and watching late night TV. He didn't even acknowledge me.

I said, "hey. You're not gonna tell my mom how to treat me anymore."

He said, "what?"

And then I described every detail of what he did to my little body for those two months before I got the private suite built downstairs. And mind you, we weren't rich. This new dude just made us barely middle class. So everybody sure found a pretty penny to make it happen, right?

I told him how I was awake those nights. I told him the counter-clockwise of his fingertip incision. I didn't have a *fuck you* in me when I was in the sixth grade, I didn't even know that his kind of touching was a thing. That was how I learned his kind of touching was a thing.

And Gary visibly shrunk before my eyes as I spoke. Old man baby fucker. He shrank to nothing in the face of my retelling. And I never really told nobody but him because he was the only bastard that needed to relive that shit. And god how he melted. He left me alone for the next year and a half of high school after that. My sister, too. And Mel couldn't possibly know what that meant to me, even now all these years later. How she gave me my power that day, how I've always known it was mine since.

So how's that same gutsy person get to be here with a narcissistic junkie "not-boyfriend" asking for anal every other day? Am I still me? Where did I go? Why I am hiding out here now on a filthy couch chewing my lip swollen with openly bleeding wounds on no less than three fingers and thirsty? So. Thirsty.

Grandma said, "don't bring a rape whistle to a gang bang," I think and pull out my phone. I can't sleep more than 20 minutes at a go without waking up fitfully and full of bad dreams so I open the porn site and decide to try and masturbate again. I never masturbated as a kid until after I lost my virginity, the sex was so fucking awful except for that it made me think *eh-o, I could do this for myself* and that was GD fantastic. I became a swift pro and double clicking the mouse and *pew-pew-pew*. I haven't looked at porn for months and it's all this incest shit at the top of the page. Jesus, what the fuck is who into and how is that Cheeto #45 somehow responsible for all these mommy issues? Gross.

I'm like three pages deep before I find a nice gang bang. Like a sexy one, where no one's mascara gets smeared and everyone is more orgy than ogre. I press my right hand down my pants after clicking the video and it's loading ... loading ... loading. Motherfucker, *redtube is down for maintenance, try one of our sister sites.* I haven't watched a porn video in three months and this is the shit I get? I almost just give up but click anyway but what I don't realize is that TS means trans porn and so now I'm into a whole scene I've been fantasizing about anyway. I watched a transwoman once in a kitchen/ wife/plumber scene and the whole thing just didn't do it for me but now I'm like *it's a sign.*

So I'm scrolling down and there's no incest shit at all which is an immediate plus and then there's no mistaking my friend Sam. *Holy Shit.* I've always heard of folks who surf porn and run across someone they know and even once a dude at the hardware store recognized me from my r/gonewild profile, but I've never never had this happen. I'm fascinated. I click.

My hand doesn't go back down my pants because somehow I don't think this is consensual. She totally hasn't given me the go-ahead on looking at her dick but I can't help myself. It's mostly just this old white dude like yelling into the phone. I don't listen to porn with the volume on so I imagine he's like making some big corporate merger or bitching at his pissy-bitch wife while my friend is in this French maid get-up just sort of moping around, no feather duster, no blue spray bottle, no sexy wiping down of clean clean surfaces. I'm like *yo babe you telling me you aint never cleaned a house before?* Her eyes are real dead too. All the non-verbals are saying she don't know what to fucking do here.

Old dude hangs up and she just gets on her knees in front of him on the floor. She keeps making confused eye contact with the camera, like who's the director here, this shit is whack! Every time her eyes meet mine through the camera, I'm a fucking Judas. He's like petting her face nicely and then just shoves his dick right in her mouth. The video is only 4 minutes long and for the first three he was on the phone while she milled about. Then he gets her to stand and kiss him and flips up her skirt enough for the big reveal that Sam's trans. Damn, her dick is nice, big and pretty. Fuck. It's rock hard, too.

Boom, scene cuts. Like *what?* Now she's perched over the black leather couch and getting drilled in the ass. Not even like the moment of penetration, which is my favorite part. But what sucks is her dick is soft now. I don't like it and I'm worried she's not enjoying it. She seems so dead, not like when we're singing karaoke together and our voices are loud and strong and everybody's laughing. Her eyes meet the camera again and I'm done. Clicked off. Guess porn's not for me after all tonight.

Rule #2 is "No Dating." Logan used to call it "100% or nothing at all." He meant about what you were into, and that's how I mean it when it comes to fucking too. Either you are friends fucking 100% or you are balls-to-bones fucking 100%. Or you are not fucking at all. There should be no confusion here, monogamous types can't be like *I'm gonna change em! They haven't met the right xyz!* Fucking assholes.

My last serious whatever partner Trevor went to jail for domestic assault against the cherry bomb he fucked after me but they got all knocked up and now there's a little baby out there unleashed on the world with him for a fuckshow lying-ass father until he took the short way out. So when she wrote me on messenger I was like "what the fuck do you possibly have to say to me?"

She just wanted to admit she was seeing how she'd prolly been lied to and the way I inadvertently convinced her I knew what she was going through was by saying the exact words he'd said to me so many nights. Words I'd never told another soul because to admit I'd gone through all that would be to admit I was a weak-ass bitch who was still being fucked hard and not saying no and blaming myself in the morning. Which I was, although we'd complicated things to be so sophisticated. I told her he said

"You spineless bitch! Fucking fight back! Stand up for yourself if you are so right about having to hide the whiskey from me!"

and

"You. Stupid. Selfish. Liar." (that one especially over and over) (then the punching of the walls and throwing you bodily into them) (then the you hiding when he is black out drunk)

Then weeping, he'd moan: *"I'm evil."*

There are more, but who cares. I taught her how to get free lawyers and the pdf and courthouse address for filing for full-custody and then he went to jail and fuck him. He gets out, gets wasted fucking drunk, loses his job at the wine bar, can't pay child support and kills himself like he's got the hard life here. Fuck him. Me n her are partners in justice now and all the fuck-asses that averted their eyes during all both our years of kick-n-poke can go fuck themselves and wear "time's up" buttons and pretend to be good when they don't know their dicks from a weapon still and that's why there is no dating allowed.

Don't give yourself emotionally up to some wanker without a thought besides *get it in without a condom on* in either of his fuck-ass heads. 100% or nothing at all, and that goes for everyone involved. Be like Sharon, I say, and she says this about her lovers: *I love them until I get what I need from them. Now you see me, now you don't.*

The fridge is blowing cold air on me and I'm already freezing and nothing has changed. Three tall boys, one 1/2 drank 2 liter, a box of old pizza. I close the door and open it again cracking one of the beers. Two tall boys now. If I lift the lid the box might be empty. I haven't heard him youtubing or texting for a half hour at least. I'm sure he's passed out drunk in there. John makes an art of being black-the-fuck-out-drunk, this one time it's after 3 am and we're in the Taco Bell drive thru and it's taking forever of course even though we're at the ghetto Taco Bell. It takes so long John passes out in the passenger seat before we've got our two 5 dollar box meals of quesarito bullshit. I pull up to the gnarly toothed white girl with a neck tattoo, for real, every girl under 22 around here has a shitty neck tattoo. I pass her $10.57 or whatever and the car dies. Fuck. She's passing me an unsweet tea and a coke and two boxes full of refried who-knows-what mush and I'm piling all that shit in a dead drunk's lap and the car is totally fucking dead. So I gather all this so-called food and then pop the driver's door and begin pushing the Camry the rest of the way out of the drive-thru and through the hair pin curve which leads to the Avenue and like the whole power steering is fucked and so I just angle her in across all the parking spots and let her rest.

I know this bitch got a crack in the anti-freeze chamber, there's the tell-tale orange smell all over everywhere I park and if I don't watch her, she'll overheat. And here we are at 3:43 am busted, broke and blackout, well him anyway. I'm just in charge of getting him and me and the tacaritos home. So I unhinge the hood and get my cell phone light out and begin investigating and sure enough the anti-freeze is just like this orange paste, and it's supposed to look like tang. And I know you can just add water to make it work for a minute so I dump out the tea and take the empty cup to the drive up window and ask the podunk boogen to fill me up with water. Twice.

I am not dressed for this time and place. I've got on a white silk tit sling and paisley brown silk genie pants all slung low around my hips and every nipple is bright as fuck headlights on and my belly is a billboard and here's me, she, alone on the side of the road broke down. Broke as fuck.

So I'm letting the water settle into the chamber and the hood is up and this brosef pulls up in his four door four wheel drive lifted nazi-mobile. He lumbers out and investigates the engine with the same intensity as me. He gets another water bottle out of his Chevy and pours it in my engine. None of my sensors are going off. It's like totally innocuous. Just a dude being a dude and I say, "I'm gonna try to turn the engine now."

He's in all white. Shorts, t-shirt, dark hair I don't know any other details. I didn't memorize him because I didn't pick up on the danger, but at this moment he turns and faces me and he says "no."

I freeze. I don't move an inch, I don't make eye contact. I am a post in the ground, I am an object, I am an inhuman being. What happens next is two fold: I become slightly aware again of how naked I am and he says "Get in the truck, bitch." The hood is wide open, he's unaware that John is there, passed out in the front seat. John is unaware I'm about to get abducted. John is passed out drunk and I'm frozen in the burrito lane. Everyone is driving past and not trying to look at anything happening. I'm standing at the passenger side tire with the hood raised. He's standing at the passenger side head light.

And then I walked right through him. I said slowly and deliberately, "that's not happening." And then I walked right through him like he was invisible. My heart-rate didn't increase. I didn't walk around him. I didn't make eye-contact, I didn't waver. I walked right through him and around to the driver's side and I got in all nonchalant like leaving grandma's after Sunday dinner.

And then I locked the doors and had an aneurysm. The hood was still up, so I couldn't see what he did, but I did see the Chevy truck drive away. I tried to shake John awake, no dice. I caught my breath in my heart for a close getaway. I chastised myself for the silk get-up which made me vulnerable, for the late night taco run, for the living in a poor neighborhood. And then I put the key in and tried to turn the engine.

Not even a *click click click.* Just dead. Same as this hunk-a-man in the passenger seat and now I've got to abandon one or both to make it home, which is about ten blocks away. So I give it ten and try to crank the engine again and it's a top shelf no-fucking-go with both the car and this wastoid husband both but I manage to shake a small enough amount of life into John to get him walking home and we abandon the Camry.

He's obliterated, and I'm trying to tell him about how I just walked straight through a rapist and how the car is dead and he's just confused about why I'm trying to make him walk home. We get to the Stop & Go before he takes his anger out on me.

"Fuck you, bitch! I hope you fucking die!" He falls to the ground.

Here's the truth, there wasn't no reason to take his ass seriously in that moment. So I scream at him, "FUCK you you fucking worthless trust fund son of a bitch!"

And he's wallowing on the ground wailing around like a baby in a crib and I swear I almost used my shoe like a pacifier. And he just keeps screaming "I hope you fucking die! I hope you fucking die I hope you fucking die!" And he's swimming in the yellow grass on the side of the Avenue and I wanna punch him so bad it's like a high. I wanna climb on his caterwauling lanky body and just lay into him like my step-father did to me because as a matter of fucking fact I was almost raped over two five dollar combo boxes and I lost my tea to the antifreeze chamber but I'm still carrying his coke and quesaritos.

But I don't hit him. I don't even yell at him. I don't do one god damn thing I want to do because I hate what I want to do as much as I want to do it. And he's just crying on the ground like a temper tantrum and all the crackheads are looking at us like kin and I kinda thought I was better than all this, but all this proves I aint. So I laugh in his stupid fucking face and leave him in the median.

So I walk home the back way and in the morning we pretend nothing happened and realistically, he doesn't remember any of it.

And now I'm going back and forth on trying to figure out whether *I wish he was fucking dead in there* or *not*, because if he was, I'd be free. I just close the fridge door without opening the pizza box. There's nothing left worth eating here and that feels like a knife to the heart.

No Duking in the Bed:

My middle finger is bleeding freely but it's plasma. I don't know how that works but the wound isn't so deep any veins are antagonized I guess but this pus just keeps seeping. The other two fingers are just loose strings of flesh I'm attached to. The stigmata burn on my palm is a huge bubble now that no one notices. No one is looking.

The worst part about tonight is the inside of my cheek. I've bitten it swollen and then once it's swollen you know it's like ten times easier to bite and now it's like a lollipop in the side of mouth except for instead of bubble gum flavored it's raw flesh and pain. Every time I bite down I give myself the ole cat-o-nine again which in my brain goes like this: *you already made this mistake, asshole.* The seeping taste in my mouth is indistinguishable from disappointment in myself. Indistinguishable from the taste of myself.

I remember earlier going up to the bartender and slamming my fist on the bar demanding a round for me and my boss. I was like *we're going to get fucked up!* The bartender was someone new, I didn't recognize them and they kicked me out of my own fucking job. I got all worried because I need the money especially if there is no junkie paying half the bills with me and instead fucking randos at motels on state lines. My heart lurches because I haven't been out of the house. This is not a real memory, I have not left the house. This is a dream again. I also remember a box of crackers torn apart by a dog, this part is not real. There is no dog and there are no crackers. My fat fingers are throbbing with pain, that's real. I haven't eaten still, that's real.

Tonight his car is here but it's also true I've slept. It could be he's left while I was sleeping and so I can't know if he's dead, dead drunk, or just having taken an uber, or been picked up by her, or possibly on some epically drunken walk into nowhere where he can take a snow nap, you know: *you always win a snow nap, because either you wake up or you don't!* The weave of the mustard yarn is a map across my fat cheek because the pillows have all fallen off the couch.

So now I'm awake and full of pus and seeping and I swear to fucking god I'm not gonna cry about some GD tornado across my face and life and I've made it this fucking far without anybody's help and I'll be god-damned if I call the police or the morgue or a hospital or his brother or Chase or any fucking body and most certainly not him. If he was out, he'd pick up because he doesn't want me to die any more than I want him to die, and then if I asked to go out to his party, his voice would say *yes* but his tone would be sad because he just wants to hit some new puss. Fuck. I know he wouldn't even pick up.

My fingers are dry because I spent two hours packing books and papers into reusable grocery bags and they seeped all the oils out of my life. I'm a dry bone I'm choking on. I'm a cough of splinters and I'm a dry heave gagging on nothing. I don't know where I'm moving as I'm tossing and turning on the stolen gray duvet but I do know that I keep turning the *turbo bass* up further and further because I know he hates that and if he's alive in there, this is my best chance of getting him to come out.

What's one more fingernail for the road?

This blanket is fucked up and this bed too and definitely the GD pillows, I knew that fucking first. Somebody is messing with my shit and there's no telling how long it's really been since I've been watching the change of shadows against the light behind the door frame I can't break through. He's over there, you know. He's behind the door and he's either dead or he's alive but I can't know unless I open the door but seriously why the fuck isn't he just coming out. Doesn't he have to piss? Am I missing it when I sleep? I go in and see the toilet seat is still down and the one hair drawn from my head and laid over the lip like I'm fucking Sherlocking some shit is still there.

I listen at the door. I can will my ears to hear through walls. His television is still on and I can't hear over it. It's on the Olympics with occasional interruptions about how many school shootings in the first 42 days of 2018: no one can decide if it's 7 or 18. People argue about such stupid shit. I can't hear over the constant noise and now it's a commercial for getting a better credit score.

It could be half a hundred things and it could be none of the dreams I've had and no matter how they infiltrate this now they still are only 50/50 on whether or not they are real but I can promise you the blue house is where we lived for the four years of high school plus the two before. And also, that's not where we are now. We are in the yellow house now with the arched doorways and I have installed two curtains and he has one door and he is in the bed behind that door and I know for a fact he has a gallon of R&R and plus some anyway. I also have reason to believe he might have eaten an ungodly amount of mushrooms and tongued some allotment of dilaudid or shot up again and really no telling with all his night shift mother-fuckers and SURE they put the cocaine in the purple Camry instead of the red one and you roughed them up while on the clock to be sure I could get some dope to set my serotonin right since I'm heartbroken.

I go back to my bed and promise not to look back. Two angels arrive at eventide and that's the ghost of Sharon and the ghost of Frannie and I lick their tears and borrow their salt and that's the weeping that alerts the mob of feelings and we're all stopped alive in this Sodom and I have no man to follow out because their god is not a god for women, and Lot's Wife is never named and that's how I know and so I nurse the tears of every woman born under this curse until I fall asleep.

✶✶✶✶✶✶✶✶✶

There aint no asylum here. King Solomon never did come round here. Go straight to hell, boy.

The music is so loud the windows are chittering and knocking their frost off in little snow bursts in the living room. Penguin food. The last time I actually saw him, and I love to collect lasts, I'll think of these things even when everything is fine but the last time was him coming out of the bathroom on Saturday night and being fresh shaved. Something was off. He'd done some shit with his eyebrows. As long as I'd known him his eyebrow was long and singular. But that day there were two smudges and a razor-wide straight edge strip down the middle. One smudge was almost a half inch wide, the other was nearer a quarter and also missing the top half. It accentuated the way his left eye bulged out a good bit more than his right. You didn't notice so much with such an elegant and noble mantle over the fire of his magnesium eyes, but now that he was clean it definitely looked like someone had taken a meat tenderizer only to one half of his skull and dislodged the full left half of his skull from the normal plane of a face.

I was like, "what the fuck happened here?" And he went on a normal diatribe about how I should shut the fuck up because once I shaved my eyebrows entirely off and that's true because I'm an alien and sometimes I just want the inside to match the outside and I want to feel whole and like everyone can see what they are getting into when they meet me. But the tragedy is, they do anyway. They see the whole me instantly even if they don't even know it. Like the fuck-ass ROLLY, like Wally but with an R, at that one speed dating event I went to, who just in the act of sitting down pointed to me "hey, look at that, the first person you met with immediately left."

And yunno I don't even fucking know what that meant, and I asked him and he backpedaled and basically said he had no idea but I know that his nervous energy let his subconscious talk for a second which is a damn rare thing for people to do and it took us both by surprise and neither of us wanted to own it after but what he meant was that both me and everyone who met me wanted to immediately leave.

And now there's John, who's stuck by my side more than anyone else, and he's in there dead, and that's because he'd rather kill himself than keep living with me. And I can't blame him anyway, I mean he did suffer me after I broke my leg, and I was fucking traumatized. I mean for three months I literally believed that if I walked out my front door the atmosphere would crush all of my bones to dust. John had to carry me to doctor's appointments screaming in terror and imagined pain.

The morning it happened it was me and John and Woodsy going to get Sunday brunch and I stood up to leave and then I fell down. I knew immediately what had happened, and I turned to them and said "I think I just broke my leg."

John says, "no fucking way, you just fell down. There's no way your leg is broken." But Woodsy is clutching his ears with his hands and shaking his head and mumbling with horror in his throat, "I heard it I heard it."

I just hold up my right knee and about halfway down the calf, the leg takes a hard left towards the center of the planet and that's when everybody's eyes go real fucking wide. So they rush me to the hospital and Woodsy lives nearby and he steals his roommate's car to drive to the liquor store and then the two of them keep me company in the emergency room while getting blasted on hidden cans of beer and a pint of R&R. They get kicked out of the ER obviously and then I'm all alone. But this is still a story about nice things John does for me.

I was like fucked up and they kept me in hospital for a week because compartment syndrome might mean I need my leg amputated any second and I could only scream all night in agony when I was trying to sleep because the tibia was straight broken the fuck in half and the fibula was broken in three separate pieces and no one could stay in the hospital room with me for all the shrieking from the pain. Not conducive to a healing environment. And John held my hand through it. And he carried me home, and he kept buying me ice and he lifted me into the bath the first time even though I thought it would kill me because for the next few months I was certifiably insane.

Who does that? Not the plant destroying, punk fuck sucking off his sleeping best friend. Not the lying sycophant scamming other poet's pennies after catching himself on fire. Not the guy who lied to his mom about us living together or getting married. He only fucking married me so I'd have health insurance anyways after the doctors just looked me in the eyes and said "you are going to break bones for the rest of your life." And that was nice in a John way, but fucking awful in a me way, because I'd rather turn to dust and be blown away than be some fucking charity case. He never meant to be a husband, he just wanted me to have physical therapy so I could walk again and a therapist to convince me I wasn't actually dead and I could walk over a wet surface without it killing my corpse.

That's how fucked up I was.

Maybe he liked me best when I was shithouse fucking crazy. Maybe he finally felt he had something over me. That seems like a real John thing to do.

✲✲✲✲✲✲✲✲✲✲

My clit is flaming fucking hurt because the nail on my right middle finger is too long and there's nothing to do here except masturbate and get sucked into my own mind vortex. Sometimes when Frannie's too drunk she goes on and on about demons and that shit is fucking boring. Skip it. Keep some shit to your GD self. But I've masturbated so much I can't touch myself any more and it's fucking annoying. The desk whiskey is nearly gone and I've been stuck here now over a day. I have to be at work by … early, day shift.

I haven't eaten anything, which is fine. But it makes me lose sight of time. I've been on the couch since Sunday night, I was home longer than I realized he might be finally dead. There's an ingrown hair on my right knee, and a hive on my left forehead. I can't be seen like that. I start digging into the puffy pore, my two thumbnails are perfectly shaped for excavation: blackhead, ingrown, anything. I can pick it all apart. I bring the make-up bag to the mirror in the bathroom and turn on all the lights. Draw a bath, scrub with salts, soak in vinegar, inhale tea tree, scour, abrade, heat, peel, cucumber all the fucking things.

Every part of me is inflamed. I could just open the door. I could just check and admit I can't go to work until I check. I can't do what I need to do without being sure he's alive in there. And what is so wrong with being sure he's ok? That's what a good person would do. Anyone with half a wit about them would just check, I mean you can be polite about it and everything.

Now it's less than twelve hours till the day shift at the Cajun restaurant. Home-owned type, not some bougie shit, we got chicken *ala mer* and Nasty Tio knows how to do roux like heaven and better yet he knows how to do alfredo which like only nobody can really do and even though his old gun shot wound is still seeping, we're in KC and that means Nasty Tio is your best shot at getting a cream sauce done right. So fuck it. I'm aint gonna miss work for this fuck-ass junkie motherfucker. His dick aint shit.

Fucking head shit. What? I'm gonna go work slinging Bermuda Triangles and oysters and being polite. Yep. What? So I'm gonna stay hitched up here because he keeps saying that I'm the only one and it's just me and *you you you*. And I buy it, because this is the USA and I gotta buy some fuckin thing.

Now it's after 1 am and I've gotta be at work at 10 am. He hasn't made a noise but I've investigated 8 new holes in my skin. I gotta get some sleep.

I asked John once when the moment he lost hope was. Like what a piss-off child he is, what a spoiled little nuisance, and I'm over here like, he must've been harmed somehow, he must've lost faith somewhere and this is gonna open me up to understand him and forgive him and be able to love him through all this fucking trauma. He looks off, lost in memory.

"Well, I always thought I'd be taller. Like 6'5". Big."

How can I love this person? Is this even a person? Am I really surprised? He told me about when he heard about 9/11 and how his uncle worked in NYC and his family was so worried and he went to his job at Pizza Hut in Overland Park and just screamed at all the crying people for what fuck-alls they were for caring.

"Life doesn't fucking matter, you phony fucks," he screamed at his co-workers.

I asked "what about your uncle?"

"Fuck him."

Deep as a sheet of paper, this fuck-ass.

Saturday night he sensed I was done in a new way, not in a longing way, which he knew how to work, son! But in a real-woman way done, like a lay-down-the-law way done. And he straight up asked me, "what was the moment? The moment you were done. What happened?"

And of course self-involved me is thinking he cares about what makes me happy, when the truth is he only cares about what makes me happy with him, and so I tell him about that moment in the shower when he said "I can't keep being your only source of emotional support."

And how after I realized that the reason he was the only source was because he was also the only source of my emotional trauma. So of course I went to him to process, he was the one who held me down in the night and he is the ghost inside my nightmares. Of course he's the only one who could answer for why he lied to Dolores his mother and to me for two years and even married me in a farce. He's the one who did this. I'm a bystander to his cataclysm, to his victimless crime, because baby I was all in.

But really, I should've known it was done two weeks earlier. When he told me he didn't love his daughter at all. When he told me he wished his six year old was an abortion, and no matter how blue her eyes or how high her reading level or how hard she punched the bully or the fact that she kept hitting so hard she broke that 5th grader's jaw, he didn't love her and never would, but he'd keep pretending to because he was afraid if he let onto the real deal, her grandmother would sue to get more child support than the $80 a month he was already paying.

It's 2018, bitch! $80 is a mani-pedi, not child support. And the grandmother should sue because Dolores and the father and the step-father are all fucking multi-millionaires, and no one should have to suffer, everyone should have new shoes and first class educations, but the truth is those rich fucks don't think some trailer trash fucks deserve their privilege, and that's when I should've known he'd sell me for whatever he'd get. But I aint worth nothing so fuck him anyway. One day I might look up that kid and have a real cohort, because we both know what it means to be un-fucking-loved and fucking trashed. Garbage kids.

There's a difference between garbage and trash. Garbage men are good men doing a hard day's work and coming along to pick up all the trash. Trash men are fuckers who abandon women, children and themselves and throw Hardee's bags and piss-filled Gatorade bottles out the windows of moving vehicles while picking up whores off the side of the road or Tinder before throwing them away, too.

Trash people are just looking to get what they can right fucking now and they'll do anything to get anything they can regardless of whether they want it or not, so they end up with a wife or a kid or a step-kid or a 401k or a sack of mushrooms or a girlfriend in Des Moines and they don't want to really do anything with any of it except get rid of it because those spoiled brats know better than anyone that they don't deserve one fucking thing. So they trash it all.

And maybe I should've known when Frannie told me he was a worthless fuck, and maybe I should have known when he lied to his mom about marrying me, and maybe I should've known when he threatened to kill me and my whole family in order to fully kill himself, and maybe I should've known when he lied to me about being tested for AIDS, and maybe I should've known when I knew that first day I ever saw him that he was lying about being raped by his priest-boy-scout-leader-gym-teacher. The story always changed so much.

But the truth is, I'll be lucky to know today, because I've been buying bullshit so long, I'm my own junkie now, and I'm invested in proving to the world … to me … that what I've been fighting for these three years lost is more than just some junkie using me to get by, but is some artist worth fighting for when really, he's just another limp dick sucking on mommy's tit and this silver spoon motherfucker is just biding time until he gets his big money no whammy inheritance and then he can just legit drink himself to death.

Everything in-between is him just faking life to his rich parents buying time to the funeral and acting right to stay in the will. And here I am, Lot's Wife, Schrodinger's Dummy, playing along as the bitch who blows on the dice and gets none of the payout.

God damn. I'm fucking pathetic.

✱✱✱✱✱✱✱✱✱

Now there's no sound in the house. I watch Netflix on mute with subtitles. I chew my nails relentlessly and where my lips are split now is like licking a broken knife wound open. I'm old enough to know I got raped before I lost my virginity but before I knew all that I thought those were two different things and I didn't equate them. Now I'm also old enough to know I wasn't raped when I lost my virginity but also who was I to know how things might be different. Darryl was my boyfriend and yeah he had a bad rap and all that but could he spin a tale about how everyone else was all wrong. And he made me feel like I was the only one who could see the truth in the world and boy howdy was his truth ultimate and shit.

So we're foolin around and his mom's passed out drunk and he's insisting that I'm ready like it's a movie from the 80's. And his 30 year old brother is blasting Pantera and we're in the basement and I'm 14 and there's Darryl's waterbed and it's behind this curtain he's hung across the room and brother is egging us both on and prolly his little dick was hard underneath his tighty-whities and everybody's drunk and Darryl was 4 years older than me and I definitely was not somebody who couldn't handle anything.

So brother is headbanging and talking about pounding ass and Darryl is putting his hands down my pants and tongue down my throat and this is what grown-ups do. This is what mom does with husband number six hundred and this is how I got here and how my sister got here and how Darryl and his brother got here, and animals been fuckin forever and shit or none of us would be here and so I knew that his grubby fingers shoved up my snatch meant now we were fucking and that meant I was grown. It's whatever.

He pulled me behind the curtain and wrangled my pants and panties around my legs and they were trapped together and he pushed 'em back and spit on his hand and rubbed it on the top of his cock and he shoved it in. The pain was a blast off, everybody knows the first time is gonna be like that. I couldn't struggle thank god because he had me held down so good. And he pumped and pumped and the death metal got louder and he started screaming the same way I could hear my mother through her bedroom door and I was a goddess, I was wanted and I was sure I was bleeding and it couldn't hurt more and I knew this what was made me a woman and I swallowed my tongue hard and pushed my heart back into its cage and tried to gyrate my hips like I heard you're supposed to do, but I was trapped under his body and could only lay there. Or rather float and rock, the waterbed was in high tide from our gravity.

The whole problem started because it kept going on longer than I thought it was going to. He's there humping and that's how it's supposed to be, and I'm still because I can't move because he's holding me down and all of a sudden I have to run but I know it's rude to leave before he's finished but I can't stay in this waterbed anymore and the music is giving me a migraine and I love him I know I do and we're gonna live together after high school but right now I just have to fucking run.

So I push him off of me and flip my legs off and over and away and I already have my shoes on because he just pulled my pants down and I grab my purse and I'm gone like donkey kong.

I run to his car, it's senseless, right? His keys are in the console. I don't know where I'm going and I don't know where I've been but I'm running away to nowhere because I have nowhere to go but I'm turning the ignition and squealing out and heading so far away and I get out of the curving subdivision of the suburban projects his mom lives in and I'm waiting at the light at 40 highway.

My breath hasn't caught itself, I'm pounding the steering wheel because I'm some sort of crazy person who can't even fuck right and barely knows how to drive because I'm only 14 when behind me someone is flashing their brights and honking and everything is so much louder than I ever thought it could be and my vision is blurring at the edges and the howl of everything can't be placed. It's Darryl in his brother's car.

My phone rang, the light was red. I answer.

Of course it's him.

"Fuck you, bitch! Get your fat ass back here, where the fuck do you think you are going?"

Of course I went back. I needed to get fucked right, right?

This is love, right?

That's what everything I'd ever seen told me, yunno?

✶✶✶✶✶✶✶✶✶

My best friend before I became a college drop out was a skater boy named Justin. God he was fucking gorgeous and I was like this kinda tweaked out braless charity case no one could understand. What we had in common was this: no one could touch us. After spring break he didn't come back for an extra week because he landed this gig in Fort Lauderdale doing modeling for a surf board company. He missed the whole opening chapter on infinite series. It's basically all about Zeno's paradox and that's how we thought of things. We were an arrow flung through the woods next to a tortoise and hare racing nonchalantly and a wolf jump jump jumping after grapes … grapes we all knew were rotten if only you couldn't reach them. The thing was, which we both knew better than all the other community college idiots, was that the arrow would never reach the fucking tree. If a capitalist fuck shoots an arrow into an anarchist tree, the arrow must travel half the distance to the tree, stop. Like there is a stop in the trajectory of pain. But then, it must travel half again. Stop. Half again. Stop. Half again. The paradox is the misunderstanding that we can infinitely divide all distances into more and more halves and still end up with something that can hit home. Or something that can feed us or something that isn't just lingering outside the final piercing. Like there is a purgatory we can wait in before acknowledging we are struck down.

We get fucking pierced through the heart with the arrow of pain.

So Justin comes over because he knows I'm the only one he can count on to catch him up. This is better than fucking in so many ways. We talk about how not only can you look at every problem from algebra or calculus or geometry perspective but that also you can do it from this infinite series projection. It's like how $1+1+1+…=$ infinity. Or more interestingly equals pi or e or the speed of light or the confluence of heart dysrhythmias. And Justin is on the floor of my bedroom with me and inventing how you can see derivatives as sums-of. It's just a lovely rearrangement of principles. It all adds up to the same thing.

And we'd sit in the back of the Calc III classroom and invent LaGrangians and were mostly wrong but sometimes surprisingly intuitive about things and now I don't wanna fuck anybody who won't invent mathematics from scratch or take an entire room's attention with a fit or wear lacy underwear over their dick.

John won't even balance his checkbook, because he knows his mom will. When I checked the mail today he had a big package from UMB, it has his and Daisy's name on it, because how else can his mommy dearest transfer him money when he needs it without a clear shot into his bank account. I wonder how many times a day she checks up on what he's spending her money on.

But realistically what only matters is what Godel taught us and that is this: you think you have the whole picture but you don't. There's always a bigger picture and it's always gonna stomp on your head if you believe you are always right but if you instead say "my nose will grow now" and pretend you are Pinocchio then you'll be a proper liar and win your certificate for being a teacher and not have to let everyone find their own way. Godel said "there are true statements which cannot be proven true" and he's right.

✷✷✷✷✷✷✷✷✷✷

My eyes flash awake and it's imperceptible because I'm used to hiding myself so fucking well. I'm pretending to be asleep now and I'm still. There's sound from his room. It's a TV show, I think it's Bojack Horseman or Big Mouth but I can't tell because I don't watch that shit. He's awake. At least awake enough to press play on the Netflix sleeper screen. There's no way that was an accident. He's not dead.

He's not dead. If he's not dead and we're broken up then what the fuck am I supposed to do? I have to go find another love, another future another whatever is in the future and I'm not totally sure anyone else could handle everything that I am and that's why I need this half-dead motherfucker in the bed behind the door I won't open because this is the best I deserve. Who can put up with this psychotic horrowshow of know-better-could-do-better 12-step GD son-of-a-you-are-a-fucking-whore.

I used to always argue that the wave function must collapse because that's how energy gets changed into matter. I mean mass times the speed of light squared equals energy and that means that there must be a phase transition, right? Yeah now I'm like fuck that, everything is matter and energy simultaneously and we're all traveling light times itself and that makes more sense than God or a flat earth or any ethics some charlatan with snake oil's got. Schrodinger tried to tell us not to try so hard. Mr. Schrodinger and his GD cat. We shoulda never opened the box because before you touch something everything is possible and afterward you're stuck with what ya got. You know that Pandora closed her box before hope could escape? The one thing she didn't loose upon the world.

Anyway, once you look in the box it's all fucked and you can't unsee what you've seen and you can never really know for sure what was going on before you opened the door. Suddenly reality exists and before we could have just *la-tee-da-ed* our way past the curtains for our Sunday best dress and have another cigar, we're gonna go far and all of that. Pandora opened the fucking box, Eve opened the fucking box, and here we are all totally fucked.

God I hate myself and I can't tell if it's because I'm trying to save him or if it's because I'm trying to save him.

I went out Saturday night because like now I'm single and shit. So the guy at the bar is going on and on about "why on earth didn't that 'date-rape' girl just fucking leave" and like "where's the line of personal responsibility" and he gets it and all but like "at what point does a woman just like stand up and say *No!*" he just *totally doesn't get why she doesn't just say no!?* And this is the kind of guy I'd especially like to eviscerate but I let him get one more sentence out. He goes on to say "I think there's like some kind of fundamental problem in the world with people just being honest." I know that's right.

So here's my opening. I have a v neck on and move my elbows to my navel so the cleavage goes nice and round. He's not listening to a thing now. I mouth a couple platitudes which draw his attention to the supplication of my lips. He's stopped listening to me long ago and has started devising exit strategies because all these motions are non-verbally indicating to him that he's for sure gonna get some. But I'm playing him like a marionette and have the least intention of pleasing him. He keeps prattling on about emotional content being devoid of logical content and about perpetuating gender norms by portraying victim roles.

"So," I say, "what women are really missing is the basic factual biological imperative that the man who scares them the most is also the one who will scare off others the most and is therefore the one most likely to be able to protect her the best. Right? It's like millions of years of the way things are."

He's so fucking happy to nod in agreement. He says, "exactly right."

And I say, "so you admit you are a natural born predator?"

He demures, *coy*. His eyes flit up at me because he didn't expect an adversary. He expected a blowie.

I say, "tell me how you get women to do what you want."

And I swear, I didn't have my hand on it, but his dick went so limp right there. And I lost my chance to make a relationship with anyone, again, because I don't care to do things in that civilized of a way.

If anyone's gonna bite, it's gonna be me.

✷✷✷✷✷✷✷✷✷

I can't sleep. Why do I let him fuck with my head like this? Boundaries, ok! Still, I'm lucky my parents are dead, they can't hurt me anymore. His mother is a whole nother story. I think she has a reverse Oedipal. What's it called when a mother wants to fuck her son? She wants to fuck him in the biblical way, and that means sexually but also emotionally. Want might be a strong word. Compelled might be better. I always imagine what she must have suffered to think her son was better off for her hand slappings and regular weigh-ins, for her picking up and dropping off of his laundry as though he was 19 still, for her two hour telephone calls every Sunday and once during the week. He would say she was a quintessential Spanish woman. She does drink a lot of wine. I don't think the Spanish would claim anorexia and guilt as their guiding principles, but what do I know, I'm midwestern. Her name is Daisy, but I think she gave herself that name, she probably has a real beast of a first generation immigrant name like Josefa Pilar or Dolores. Dolores means "sorrows" I decided to call her that from the first meeting on.

Their family is a testament to the horror of wealth. Million dollar homes, ten rooms each fully stocked with a bevy of cold emptiness. Three dens and two playrooms for future grandchildren and the one that no one knew existed till three weeks ago because the underage meth addict who got knocked up by John lied to some other fellow that he was the dad. It would be two years before a paternity test, a felony conviction, a custody trial and then a sample of John's blood sent three states away and BOOM new papa to a now 3-year-old-girl. Merry Christmas everyone! But when I met Dolores over Thanksgiving dinner, it was a full house built for empty people and she only said that she was surprised I sounded "ghetto."

She actually told a story of how brave she was to go down to *Armordale* and serve meals to the poor and homeless people who live west of downtown on the Kansas side. Her husband interjects *we kept Daisy in the back, though, those men can be very dangerous.* He's all puffed up and forks another bite of chewy Chicken Parm into his fat face melted under his hair plugs. Armordale is the exact neighborhood I grew up in, John saw the house and wept. Fucking unsafe. Here in gated suburbia is where I'm unsafe. The white man of European descent is the global apex predator. Nothing should make you shake in your boots more than a white dude in a business suit walkin up on you with a briefcase and a smile on his face.

After dinner, over scotch naturally, after I was reprimanded for getting the vintage Baccarat highball for my Laphroig 15 and informed how those aren't "guest" glasses. John had spiked pungent with a small fear when he saw me choose the glass, he told me *no*. I said *these are for drinking, it will be fine.* He was right, I was wrong. I have been wrong about most things, but I don't experience shame. I think the world is wrong because that glass feels so good in the hand, the *pring* of the large square cube of ice against the impossibly melodic crystal sounds so good, how could anyone not take such pleasure? Just leave it on the shelf for the dust? Fuck that.

Theirs is a world of obedience to tradition. Mine is a world of *fuck you.*

I'm jealous, there's no two ways about that. I wish I had a financial planner and loving parents and if somebody, anybody had been there to navigate me into brightness and a real college, I'd have been fucking curing cancer and shit, I'd be like Elon Musk's girlfriend and we'd habitate Mars ethically and shit, and instead of all that I'm a community college drop out fucking a junkie who's dead or not dead in the next room which is another way of saying he's dead or just avoiding me in the next room and what good is any of that shit?

I mean my mom wasn't ever shit in my life, and my grandpa was, and my long dead dad was, but my aunt was the one who made me feel like I was even worth a shit. But my aunt was like this fuck-up right? And she did all kinds of drugs with her 16-year-old kid and so when he got to 17 and a half, he was like feeling full of himself and he did a LOT of fucking drugs and he came home because he thought his mom was cool with it and she was. So this particular night he comes home at 6 am and she's waiting up for him and he's nodded out and he passes out on the couch and she passes out on the chair next to him and she's like fuckin old and she's never really seen anybody OD or anything and she just passes out next to him. Cool. Then she wakes up in the morning and starts hem-hawing about pancakes or microwave sausage biscuits and the house is silent. Silent.

They're all sorta musical so this is weird. And I can only imagine, but what I know is fact is that she went back to the mustard weave couch in the front room and

boom

dead son on the couch in the front room. This is what you need to understand: she knows she fell asleep and slept through his last breath. She didn't think he was that high. She knew he'd be fine in the am and she was so fucking wrong. Dead as fuck. 17. Whatever. I'd never be as much as he was in that cold sore spot. And then of course she had to follow in his footsteps.

Asked Carl Sagan how stars die, he said 'usually an overdose.'

What the fuck man, I just wanna live over here OK? It's all too fucking much for me. No dying allowed. I didn't ask to be born into a world of death, I didn't ask to live in a world of wishing we were dead. I didn't sign on to a contract of just being resigned to whatever I don't understand or whatever I was willed into. Fuck all of you. I have a library and in it is *Man's Search for Meaning* and in that Frankl says: "The one thing you can't take away from me is the way I choose to respond to what you do to me. The last of one's freedoms is to choose one's attitude in any given circumstance."

Grandpa smoked until he coughed up his lungs and dad drove his car into a pole and mom's heart gave before her liver could and Auntie did drugs with everyone and now I'm an orphan and that completes his sexual fetish trifecta and John drinks with everyone and shoots up with some of them and we all drink until our livers explode and I'm drinking right now because I got the kitchen whiskey out and I need to get to fucking sleep so I can work tomorrow.

Why can't orphans play baseball? *They don't know where home is.*

 ✶✶✶✶✶✶✶✶✶

Friday night there was a punk show we wanted to see in Salina, Against Me!. John played *Gallant Fellow* early on, insisting he'd not drink so I could and he'd drive us the long drive home and I could have all the fun and enjoy the show. But of course Mo was passing a bottle of whiskey around and who can resist that? And then Courtney showed up all hyper-sexually-available and yunno, I really wish it was because she was affirmed and confident, but we all know it's because she's learned to use her power and this is the easiest way to do that. She's seen more dicks in an alley than men who respect her and *har har* and all that. It used to be easy for me to hate chicks like that but now I just feel sorry for them. Courtney says shit like "damn, all these pissy bitches mad I be fucking their man" and knows that buys her an all access pass to on-your-knees-backstage but baby, baby girl, let's see where we all are when you're 50. Knees give out, salt lasts. But she gives John a flask, and he's in, you know he has to take anything someone offers him, because he's so desperate to be accepted.

And then Mo and Courtney are like, *let's go to the bar!* And I'm like, *we gotta 3 hour dive home and I'm done*, but John's hellbent now. He can't even believe he's been like *invited out* and he's so fucking hard about it that there is no telling him no. In fact, there's no convincing him of the fact that none of the punk show fucks are gonna show up at the bar. They were just saying anything to get him out. So now me n him n *good girl* are at the bar and he's gotta drink harder and harder because the only other option is admitting his new "friends" aren't ever and weren't ever gonna show up. So he's buying Trumpet fucks in middle Kansas shots of fireball and yeah they're slapping him on the back sayin *atta'boy* and all that.

At one point John turns to the bartender and says "I want a pint glass filled to the rim with warm well vodka, no ice, nothing, and I don't care what it costs!" Oh how the boys laughed, and John laughed with them and I knew he was feeling himself in a way my discord and sneering lip and eyeroll could never make him feel himself. And

I was disdaining him so hard in every fucking way. Fucking piss-ant. Jesus, spineless weakling. But I know better, so I just switch to water, because I know I'm driving tonight.

The pint glass cost $47, and seriously bitch ass bartender fucking served it to him. That's fucking criminal. And they're playing pool and slamming their fists against the bar laughing about the war and their women and the world and I've never felt like more of an outcast so I both hate and am jealous of him for being able to just love these backwater racist fucks. And they aren't that right now, cuz everybody is fucking white, but I know what that flag means, and why they laugh about Pepe, and John's fitting right in because he's been listening to that crusty fuck Alex Jones and they all know the code words and they're high-fiving with the strength of what they call a hurricane but is at best a hiccough.

I go play darts alone. There's no winning this drinking game, it's just about waiting till he's worn out. I'm closing my eyes and imagining what it might be like to be an astronaut. Where is the Earth, who are meteors, asteroid my lover, sparse atmosphere, low sun two moons, I have a comet heart with an immense orbit, I'm lost a bit in nostalgia for lost futures. John paid his tab. Hey *whoa*.

I start to follow him, so discreetly. He pays his tab, $10 on $92. Fucker. He goes to the john, don't think this coincidence goes past me ever, he's King Toilet of the Trashpeople, King John. He goes outside to the smoking patio with the wood furniture. I'm a sweet little ghost, I have learned how to snoop without ever being detected, I see so much more than he'll ever catch onto. And then I fucking see him start finishing the left over drinks and beers on the patio. And there are so many of them for some podunk Kansas town, fuck!

So emerge I go and just lay into this asshole, "What the fuck are you doing!? You said you were gonna drive, we are fucking leaving right fucking now." And you know he fought me on the back patio with everyone fighting, it's goddamn typical and so fucking boring. Once Frannie said *the problem with heteros is that they mistake inconvenience for assault and that's why they fight in parking lots so much.* Get outta my head, girl. Here I am, a walking cliche. I'm just like conniving and convincing this fuck through screaming and shame that it's time to leave and time to stop fucking drinking.

I don't even really remember what happened in the next three hours except that *this is being held hostage*, trapped in the car with a drunk fucker full of testosterone. That the first hour was him screaming at me for being a bitch or whatever and then I was so fucking thankful he passed out. It was precisely 45 seconds after paying the toll on the Kansas Turnpike when the driver's side window spontaneously combusted. I'm speeding up to seventy miles per hour when *pop!* spiderweb shatter-glass the window just fucking breaks. It bursts in on me, showering me with tiny irregular squares of thick glass suffusing me with micro-cuts and sticking in my hair and jacket and sweater. I gasp. He wakes up. He's got his wind back.

"What the fuck did you do you fat fucking cunt!? You're gonna fucking pay for that, bitch, pull over and let me drive." John is still nearly black out drunk, I can tell, and I also know that I'm gonna be fucking killed if I don't pull over, I reached for the scarf around my neck unconsciously. It's not there. I know just how to calm a violently angry man down, every woman does. And this is where all my practice playing dumb comes in. You know how many exits I "accidentally" missed and went by? Just the opposite of Know-It All-Nelly, I'm Know-Nothing-Jelly because jam sticks its dick all the way in, *amiright?* And I'm just a soft spread, right? Stupid, submissive bitch.

I finally pull over and with my gagging heart pass over the keys to John. He's 6'5" right now for sure you know? He's got all the power now, he's gonna get his way and what he wants is to drunk drive us home to KC. And that's what he does while I collapse into myself and surrender my mind and needs to the needs of another man and that's when his dick gets real real real hard. And that's when he grabs me by the nape of my hair and shoves my face into his jeans. I don't know how to breathe between his gut and the steering wheel, he shows me I don't need to breathe.

"Unzip me bitch." I do it.

"Suck my dick, bitch." I do it.

"Swallow my cum, bitch." I try to do it.

But somehow, I can't swallow, I'm gagging, I dying between my mouth full of his dick and my throat full of his cum and I can't fucking swallow it and because I can't swallow it, I also can't fucking breathe and this is how I'm going to fucking die. He's holding my head down for one last thrust and I'm choking to death my eyes are burning and tears are sheeting down my face and I can't breathe and my whole body begins struggling against his hand on the back of my neck. I fucking donkey kick the passenger window right the fuck out and he lets go screaming again.

"You fucking bitch! You are paying for both of these windows!" He slurs. And now we're driving this fucking Toyota Camry with busted driver and passenger windows both, one spontaneous and one because I kicked it out and then turned my mouth to the highway and spit all his cum into the wind. My body is black hole cold and my throat is sandpaper as I tremble into the corner of the seat farthest away from the junkie. I start checking my body for injuries *did I break my leg kicking the window?* My shoulder is bruised from the wheel, neck cricked and chirping, I lost a contact from the crying and pushing against the jean of his leg, I need water for my throat, my jaw is sore, I'm barely bleeding from a hundred little cuts on my cheeks, shoulders and legs. I'm so tiny in the corner of the seat and my body wishes to disappear, imagines leaping out onto the highway receding and receding. My stomach turns and I vomit out the window.

Something about my coughing and gagging over broken glass softened him.

Unbelievably we got stopped in a DUI checkpoint on the Avenue six blocks from home. He handed his ID over and offered condolences to the cop for having to deal with nitwits. I fucking prayed he'd be arrested. I almost told. He'd have blown like a 1.4 or some shit. He'd have gone to jail and I could've walked home. But no, the cop just chuckles with this fucking huckleberry and tells us to have a good night.

John turns to me and says, "it's good to be white."

I'm trying to remember through the whiskey, the sleeplessness, the dissociation and self-hating haze the order of events. What's even real? The car windows were Friday night, Saturday morning we broke up and he got in his busted ass car in the negative nine degree temperatures and met at least two DTF women to get his *swerve* on with before afternoon. I took a nap and haven't seen him since. I went to the bar Saturday night and then it was another fucking wasted Sunday because we were too fucked up to act like decent human beings and what the hell even happened to Monday and now it's Tuesday morning and he's contained in the box of what used to be our bedroom and I have to go to work in like four hours.

All I have to show for everything is a bit of loose nail on my thumb. That when I lick my lips it's all salt from so much crying. The pillow is shifting. I've wasted two whole days waiting for him. Waiting for me to stop waiting. I can't walk out the door as long as he's in there, *what would Seabeck do?* He'd run in and pull John down from the rafters and tear a hole in the plastic bags he's sealed over his head with a duct tape bow tie. John would take a deep breath and live instead of dying. Seabeck'd pull another bottle of scotch out of a bag and say *it's too late now little brother.* But then he could leave, I can't leave. I can leave. I don't know why I can't leave. I have to leave. My cheek hurts. The burn blister is burst. I pick at the scabs on the thousand tiny glass cuts.

I'm an army of me waging a war of attrition against myself.

✶✶✶✶✶✶✶✶✶✶

The repeater thoughts are on parade, marching up and down my brain pan both indignantly and with tremendous righteous pride. *I hope you fucking die, bitch* is always the ringleader. *Stupid, selfish, liar* is always at the tail end. *Shut the fuck up you fat bitch* has its own banner that shows thin me next to fat me and remembers how people treat you like a fucking goddess when you are thin. It's like everyone is happy to see you and everyone wants to know you and and buy your drinks and open your door. But mostly they just see you. Eye contact. And when they look at you, they want you. Now I'm invisible. *Nother round barkeep!* I don't know if it's for a fight or a beer and a shot. Frannie tells me I'm supposed to not give a fuck about all these people. She's fucking thin and beautiful though, she doesn't know. Fuck her. She's had chlamydia more often than teeth cleanings and doesn't even have one great love to show for it.

Her teeth are fucked up, by the way. Like she could chomp a bit like a horse does, I tell her she should be a bridle and a pony-tail butt plug and make a fortune on fetish channels, being she likes to fuck so much anyway. She doesn't think this is funny one bit and actually she doesn't even like to fuck, she just wants attention and to feel she has value. She's embarrassed admitting it, but she knows, like deep inside her knows that the only way anybody's gonna love her is if she does anal, fucks like a dirty whore and can deep throat like the porn stars and never never fucking puke on a cock. Unless that's their thing, yunno?

Once she demonstrated to me how to practice killing your gag reflex. John knows how to do this, too. She gets her tooth brush and sits back down on the vintage couch with the massive plants on either side and the hand-made coffee-table laden with rare Playboys from the 70's which clearly indicate how "sex-positive" she is for all her *johns*. She waddles in on her knock knees and sits criss-cross-applesauce. She looks me dead in the eye, *dead eye* being the operative words, and plunges the non-bristly end all the way down her throat, just barely holding on to the head. She holds it there and rolls her eyes away and then begins fucking her own mouth with it.

The plastic goes impossibly deep in and out, and she's so right: nothing is happening to her. It doesn't matter in the least. She rolls her eyes back to mine and I'm just a bit under-impressed and not at all as slack-jawed as one of her partners must be. I wonder how many times she's performed this feat of majesty for her dates as part of small talk.

"After you can do that, then use bigger things. You can also just practice with your fingers anytime. I do it everyday after I brush my teeth, because you have to do it over and over to make the gagging stop."

In the back of my head I know that she and John both actually got so good at deep throating from doing it after every time they eat if you catch my drift, and I've learned to recognize the tooth decay in other people, too. Lots of skinny bitches got some hella sicko teeth. Mine are big as chicklets and really fucking strong and if you stick your hand or your toothbrush or your cock too far down, I'm not gonna puke, I'm gonna bite.

Kurt Godel, Carl Sagan and Nikola Tesla all were afraid of swallowing. Godel believed people would poison him for being a German during the war of the bomb. Tesla saw critters in a microscope, and was like *fuck all that shit, ain't none of that goin in mah mouth.* Sagan was afraid that once the food was chewed he wouldn't be able to swallow it. That's the most interesting one to me, the others kind of make sense, germs and poison are all outsiders mangling your life, but Sagan is much more sublime. He's afraid of himself, of his body betraying him. He's afraid of what's closest to him. That makes sense to me. These transcendent monoliths of men, brought to skin and bones by the simplest and most necessary act of being alive: eating.

Sometimes I think they knew everything they consumed got sooner or later used against them and the phobia was the embodiment of their fear of their work. Tesla famously ran huge amounts of electricity right through his body, he holds a lightbulb in his hands and it glows. Sagan recreated life in a lab with radiation of amino acids, fucking radiation man, it eats you from the inside out. And Godel, my sweet logician honey-bunny? The greatest thinker of all time? (After Poincare, obv.) He nearly got charged with treason because at his naturalization hearing no one could talk him out of telling the judge how he'd discovered a loop-hole in the US constitution which could allow a legal way for the state to become fascist. He explained in great and boring detail to the aghast judge and made numerous comparisons to the historical precedence of how the Weimar Republic also turned to the *Deutsches Reich*. Fortunately our kooky friend Einstein was along for the ride and vouched for his best friend. Fat finger Albert.

Then Godel went on to prove that all of our mathematics was just a pale imitation of something we hoped to call truth, because he never learned that people don't like to be called out on their shit.

							✴✴✴✴✴✴✴✴✴✴

The morning is starting to color the street behind the slatted blinds. When I get up from the couch it feels like my leg is broken, but it's not. At least I'm walking around, so it must not be. It feels like it is though. I limp into the bathroom and preen my ear at his door. It's quiet in the bedroom. The hair on the toilet hasn't moved. It's surrounded by little shaved bits of squirrelly pubes and looks like a three-month-old Christmas tree from an orphanage.

My earliest memory is Christmas at my aunt's house and there's a bike behind the tree. It was a big frame banana seat and tassels from the handlebars which I called streamers then and it was royal purple and had a rainbow across the white seat and it was a three speed with handle brakes so you could pedal backwards meaninglessly as you cruised and I loved that. I rode that bike until my aunt died. I rode that bike until I turned sixteen because I never really could get the hang of the infinitely cooler skate-board, but I still wanted to keep up with everyone. Then I got a car and now I don't even remember one thing about what happened with that bike and that's life, yunno?

The worst part of getting off the couch will either be finding him dead or finding him not dead. Either way I'll be finding myself completely alone and he already has a string of other needy chicks banging on his door and I'll be meaningless and worse that means I was meaningless before all the whole while that I was giving my whole heart to this whatever the fuck this is. He's hung onto me until he got his first car and now I'm gathering dust in the garage. Like I wasn't a great ride. Like I've thought about that old bike needing oil and an alignment since the day I got the keys. It's in everybody's nature to take what's faster and sleeker and just throw everything else in the trash.

When I go in there, either thing that happens means I will be in the trash. The trash of his life. Now I'm recyclable, now I'm damaged goods. And I know I won't be able to find someone after, and I know this piece of shit is my best shot and any walking away is like walking into the desert away from the water and believing in mirages and willingly putting my whatever emotional trauma as more important than being loved. Seriously, I know in the aftermath I'll know that love is the thing that can't be had again, and you can fight and you can fuck making up but once you stop making up then you are dead in a whole new way.

You've got to be sexually available to keep his attention, to keep a shit-hole of people's attention anyway. The same people who can't be straightforward, the same people who want to kill a motherfucker for jaywalking, the same people who can't go one minute without 100 text messages and constant attention, and *pleasure center* baby.

Pleasure Center, Baby! You gotta keep those rocks hot and ready. One time in the beginning John asked me to be his flesh masturbation if his afternoon date wasn't DTF. It's like getting out that rainbow banana seat bike from the garage and riding it with your too long legs and wondering how it could have been so perfect for you before. And I'm just the used toy. Unless of course I upgrade to a baby powder royal blue Nissan Versa with fucking paddle shifters and leather interior. But I'm two wheels, I require balance and acumen. I'm handle breaks that'll stop you so fast you flip over the handlebars if you don't know how to gracefully stop. I'm a thumb shift and an audible clinking of chains for distance and I'm the choke of uphill.

I liked to go uphill on that bike, and I learned how to stand upright while pedaling hard and using my hands to push the body of the bike hard left and then hard right in synchronicity with the hard push of my feet and I don't know if it was true but it made it seem like the hill was so much easier to climb.

The fucking truth of all this bullshit is that at the bottom line I'm an unlovable fuck and everyone knows it and I know it and only I won't swallow it. The proof is in the pudding, baby doll fuck ass. Just add shit up. And it aint pretty, bitch. You are the product of a one-night stand. You were given into the hands of aunts and aunties and grandparents from day one so your Sharon Tate look-alike mother who was all of 21 could go out and get her swerve on. Like she was after something meaningful or lasting or anything other than just placating her immensely tiny need to feel beautiful and wanted. Wanted. That's the thing I'm not, maybe it's romantic to call it unlovable. So quit your crying.

Of course everybody wants to fuck me. Duh, some don't, some do and some take it and sometimes I scream and sometimes I survive and the thing I'm pissed about is the next fucking day. The next fucking day when everyone is just after the next spread legs and if I'm telling you (me) the truth then the truth is I'm afraid that all my build-up about being better than my mother is just so much delusion and this motherfucker has just bought into all my issues to get a real good lay. I'm a real good lay if you pretend to love me. And if this junkie doesn't love me? Then he's not dead he's just faking being dead he's just avoiding me. Maybe if he is dead then he really loved me after all. Maybe he's trying to save me from him and all this. All these thoughts are just like being seven-years-old in the garden tearing a flower apart petal by petal *he loves me he loves me not*.

Schrodinger took his cat to the vet, he said 'I have good news and bad news'.

One time I asked to be left alone and instead he chased me all around the house. He finally let me sleep alone on the couch but I woke up with him next to me and holding me so fucking tight. It reminded me exactly of what Gary would do to me when I was 12. My heart started racing and I was fucking twelve again and couldn't move an inch and couldn't do anything and then I was like FUCK. THIS. and went to the bed and slept there. My heart didn't stop racing though and I had nightmares all night about having to stab white man after white man in the chest with an endless set of kitchen knives so that I could get out of this room alive.

I woke up again and now he's holding me down in the bed and this time he has a raging hard cock pressed into the cleft of my ass. Then I really couldn't move. It's exactly like so many other times and it's always a man I fucking know, it's always a man I fucking love somehow and why do they get so fucking hard when they are holding me down and why can't I just get the fuck up and leave? If they loved me they wouldn't hurt me and if hurting me makes them happy then it's proof I'm unlovable.

It's the nail in the coffin and I'm buried alive.

✶✶✶✶✶✶✶✶✶

He loves me he loves me not has been added to the repeater thoughts, it's ok. Last week after the tires debacle I went to the bar to get drunk and I went to the bar I knew Sharon would be at. I tell her I need some advice. I can't say yes and I can't say no to John. I can't live with him and I can't live without him and I can definitely hate myself more deeply and I definitely can never tell anyone about the truth of all that but for whatever reason I decided I was gonna tell Sharon. Sometimes when I have a really hard decision, I just let someone else make it for me.

So I told her the whole truth, and she guffawed in the way only old women can do when faced with a young person's deep pain that makes the baby feel both ok and fucking stupid and maybe capable of change. She put her gnarled knuckles on my shoulder and said "baby, you can't love a man more than he loves himself, he'll just drag you down with him." And that's why I broke up with him after Friday night.

"I've never loved anyone more than they love me. Don't do it."

She's prolly had more pleasure in life than anyone I've ever met and being met with her disdain and humor in that moment made me feel like I could fuck any and everyone with nothing but flexing pleasure. And I know I've been loving John more than he loves me. I know he's been lying to everyone about me and his taxes and his parents have a false address concocted in a concoction with his friend Hunter because they both think it's cute to lie to everyone about who they are even though they both actually have hearts of gold and are just really afraid of being seen completely.

But the point of this is that Sharon doesn't tell anybody what to do. So when she laughed and told me to leave, I knew that was something I couldn't say no to. It'd be like murdering her so she wouldn't save me. I don't want *duende*. Maybe I need to be saved right now, and maybe I knew exactly who I needed to tell me a terrible truth. Sharon always told me that you hear the truth in the form that you are comfortable with, and that's why she always saw the Virgin Mary, because she was raised Catholic. But I wasn't raised anything, so maybe what I need is Sharon.

Sharon's salon is usually full of suburbanites and she's there, totally unappreciated, except by me, and so once in awhile I go and this night everybody is hum-drum-ho-ho rudderless and I'm biting at my nail and doodling in the margins of a comment card. Sharon's laid back like a full snake, or a real 1%er, like somebody who's got something over on you. Cat that got the canary in the coal mine and did anyone survive, we have no fucking idea. And everyone's going around talking about their *creative process* and I'm rolling my eyes so hard underneath the brim of my ball cap because I aint trying to act all superior either but seriously this whole conversation is more about the excuses everybody convinces themselves of to *not* create. It's just a bunch of wankers who like to say things like *I like to fancy calling myself an artiste* with a fucking accent mark and everything.

They don't know the first bleeding thing about ravishing your soul and gnawing the bone of the poison you ate but maybe actually are. They haven't poured a bleach bath or scrubbed bedbugs or fucked a dirty kid on an abandoned mattress in an alley, they've graduated college and gotten good jobs. And I'm sure some super-genius could write a great story about boredom and predictability but all the geniuses I know would rather die in a chainsaw juggling accident than slurp down company coffee calculating the hours of shits they took on the clock. Fucking tourists writing emails. They just like to play at this life so they can seem edgy and cool over the water cooler vending machine daily meeting wtf ever even happens in office buildings during office hours, because I don't actually know at all.

And so this one's busy with the church fund drive, and that one's busy with helping his grandkids, and he's been having writer's block and I'm over here at like full-pitch fever of self-abusing-wondershow eating myself alive because destruction is hungry. Whatever. I know in these kind of situations it's better if I don't say a word because nobody likes their nose being rubbed in shit and anyways I'm just here to drink and see my Mama Shiva. So I dig the pencil lead into my raw cuticle for the pleasure of the sensation next to all this dead weight.

The momentum of the conversation moves to Sharon, and if possible, she sits back a little more. Her black pants are polyester and unironed, pilled. Her shirt, an over-washed wide horizontal stripe, her teeth, rotten and crooked, her tits swinging so wide across her chest. She surveys the tourists as only a lifer can do.

"Now that I'm old, I just try to stay out of my own way."

God damn, bitch. You old bitch. You just give it all away don't you. Fuck. She been savin that for me, or would I have missed it if I hadn't come out tonight? *Just stay out of your own way.* It's every pop-psyche mental-health chin-up cliché but made into something that whips you with silken grit. How do you stay out of your own GD way? Two blinks. How am I already in my own way.

And what she's really saying is that you gotta figure out on your own who's dead and who's still living.

✳✳✳✳✳✳✳✳✳✳

The pillow is back. I have to work. I can't miss work. I have to leave. The sun slashes through the blinds like a warning bell. There's a sudden extra pain in my hand. I look at the disgusting, bitten and ripped nails, and inexplicably, salt has begun to grow there like the water of me is dissipating and all that remains is this ancient dead sea where everything floats and nothing can drown and everything is full of rage. I'm home.

Here is the deep growing expanse of me surfacing. I think I've died again. This is dying. The back of my hands crystallize, and the salt expands. It's growing out of the palm whorls, the wrist lines which indicated once to a fortune teller that I'm a hard worker, there are many of those lines crossing and slashing at the latitudes of my wrists. I'm sitting criss-cross-applesauce and my heart just stops altogether.

The house is completely silent. Even my breathing is finally stopped.

I couldn't be happier about this, thank you body, a stasis. A doing of absolutely nothing, a having of no intentions, *I love you. Hello, it's me, I'm happy.* I'm so completely dead.

The torn edges of my fingernails have stopped bleeding, the salt is absorbing everything. It's to my elbows, it's to my neck. I can taste its pungent kiss on my lips and it's good. My toes begin to crust over, the sandman is dusting my eyes shut, matting my eyelashes and ear holes and nose until I don't even breathe anymore and I'm so dead here, thank you, thank you God. I can feel the salt leeching into the bones into the marrow. It hurts. This is the wound. Here is the wound at the center, where I was abandoned. Here is where he took me without permission. Here are the gravestones of my family. Here is no one coming to get me, here is being unheard and unseen, here is the cold dinner table and the food dried to the plate, here is the packing of snow into an igloo for a child, here is the wound at the center and the salt is eating the scabs there, here is the freezing water filling the cracks in the walls, I'm so so still my body cakes in the white firmament.

The sunlight is evaporating me. I am not the obelisk of salt unable to leave the couch. The water of my body has given up the vessel. It whirls in the fresh cold draft of the house around what's left of me. The sun heats us and the clouds of me form in the atmosphere of the room, I'm airborne. A storm in the cage. Somehow the water and the salt of me has separated. John will think I was only salt, but Sharon knows I was always water.

The eyes of the rain look back on what it left behind in the sea of me, a body of salt. This is the nature of the womb, things must be rent apart. Things which began as the pain of having been separate or the pain of having never been met. I divorce myself in the heat of the cold. There is a rendering of fat from meat. The part of me that leaves on the wind says goodbye to the part of me that stays spread-eagled on the couch and looks back. The part that looks back leaves Las Vegas to the dreams and she has lovely fingers. She opens the door. That part looks back, leaves a pillar of salt in the living room, leaves this all behind.

The cloud of me thunders to the dead or not dead man in the other room:

It was a pleasure to meet you.

also by **Jeanette Powers**

(poetry)

Dandylion Riot

Heaven We Haven't Yet Dreamed *(split)*

Sparkle Princess vs Suicidal Phoenix

America Stabbed James T Kirk in the Arm with a #2 Pencil

Perfectly Good Muses: the collected apologies of Jeanette Powers

Dead Things I Excrete *(secret book)*

Gasconade

Don't Lose Your Head

Beautiful Earthworms & Abominable Stars *(split)*

Cosmic Lost and Found *(split)*

Novel Cliche

Tiny Chasm

Earthworms & Stars

Absolute Futility

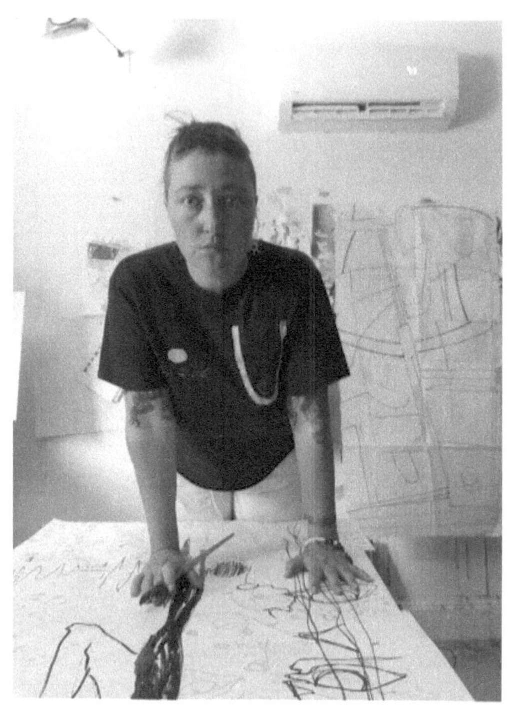

Jeanette Powers is a non-binary queer artist, working class anarchist and swimmer of rivers. They can be found petting stray cats and wishing on the first star of the night wherever there are nights and cats. As long as the clouds are clear. Powers has been published widely as a poet, and *Victimless Crime* is their first novel. They ran a generative performing arts venue in Kansas City MO for six years, facilitating hundreds of live, original shows before gentrification ran the artists out and Powers became a Dandylion Riot. This is because the powers-that-be can pave the world and artists will endlessly crack the pavement, sending their green shoots, bright sunlight flowers and wish-worthy seeds across the gray. No one can stop dandylions. They are also the founding editor of Stubborn Mule Press and an organizer for FountainVerse: KC Small Press Poetry Festival. Follow them on IG @dandylion_riot .